COME MORNING

COME MORNING

LESLIE DAVIS GUCCIONE

Carolrhoda Books, Inc./Minneapolis

Adventures in Time Books

Text copyright © 1995 by Leslie Davis Guccione
Jacket illustration copyright © 1995 by Ken Green

This book is available in two editions:
Library binding by Carolrhoda Books, Inc.
Soft cover by First Avenue Editions, 1997
c/o The Lerner Publishing Group
241 First Avenue North
Minneapolis, MN 55401 U.S.A.

Guccione, Leslie D.
    Come morning / by Leslie Davis Guccione.
      p. cm.
    Summary: Twelve-year-old Freedom, the son of a freed slave living
in Delaware in the early 1850s, takes over his father's work in the
Underground Railroad when his father disappears.
    ISBN 0-87614-892-5 (lib. bdg.)
    ISBN 1-57505-228-8 (pbk.)
    [1. Underground railroad—Fiction. 2. Slavery—Fiction. 3. Afro-
Americans—Fiction.] I. Title.
PZ7.G9344Co 1995
[Fic]—dc20   94-48003

Manufactured in the United States of America
2 3 4 5 6 7 – BP – 02 01 00 99 98 97

With love
For Wilmington Friends School
especially the late Justine Woodall
and Ambrose Short
who made me read,
Sarah Longstreth, who made me write,
and my classmates
who made me one of them

AUTHOR'S NOTE

Although this story is entirely my invention, the setting is real. Isaac and Dinah Mendenhall, John Garrett, and Harriet Tubman were heroes of the Underground Railroad and might have used the same route Freedom Newcastle followed.

Many thanks to the staff at the Wilmington Friends School library, Hagley Museum, the Eleutherian Mills-Hagley Foundation, the Brandywine Valley Tourist Information Center, and my parents, Edward and Winifred Davis, for their help with research.

I'm also grateful to Nancy Barlow, current owner of the Mendenhall house, who gave me a tour, showed me secret passageways and helped me imagine how it might have been that spring night in the early 1850s.

Freedom Newcastle yanked his grandmother's quilt off his pallet bed. The patched-and-passed-down coverlet was worn soft as flannel and would lull him to sleep in no time. Instead he lay right down on the rough mattress ticking and let the cornhusk and straw stuffing poke him. He was twelve years old. Pap could make him go to bed, but Pap couldn't make him sleep.

Free crossed his arms over his chest and stared soldier-straight at the shadows that wrapped the roof beam just over his head. He needed to stay awake. He needed the poke and jab of an uncomfortable mattress.

He'd spent the whole day trimming willow. He had chopped the spring saplings into four-foot lengths, stripped them, and stacked them in the back of the wagon, ready for delivery to the Hagley Yards. Willow work demanded a full night's sleep, but Freedom Newcastle was determined not to get one.

"Good night, son," Nehemiah Newcastle called up the loft ladder.

"Pap—"

"Don't dwell on it, Freedom. The less you know, the safer you'll be. I promised your mama when she died."

"That's all you ever say!"

"That's all you need to hear."

"Mama meant I wasn't to help while I was a child." He opened his fingers and held them up in the dark. "I'm growed, Pap."

"Get your sleep. Come morning you'll need a heap of energy for the willow work. Good night."

"Night," Free grumbled back. Come morning he'd have missed the night's adventure...again. He rolled over defiantly, as if his father could see him from where he sat in the cabin below, next to the oil lamp.

The mantel clock ticked. Free heard Nehemiah put away the Bible. He heard him close the door softly as he went out to check on the livestock. He heard him return.

Free lay still and strained his ears for the sound of whispers or distant horses' hooves. Any whistle on the wind, any howl or hoot might be a signal. He sniffed for the faint but unmistakable odor of dog chase—turpentine mixed with red pepper. It was wrapped on shoes to ruin the scent for the tracking hounds that patrollers used to follow runaway slaves.

The dark hung on him like a weight. He imagined the soft sound of boots on the cabin floor as they were laced over bare and bleeding feet. Pap would put his finger to his lips as he stood at the fireplace. He'd hold a candle over a crude map, then throw it in the embers. The flame would waver and flicker. The glow would move over the room below, then out to the privy behind the barn, as Pap risked everything to see another runaway safely through his station. Free knew that Pap was an Underground Railroad conductor. Or maybe he was even a stationmaster, hiding the runaways right out on their property.

Free had imagined it a thousand times. If he could just stay awake long enough to hear...Fatigue pressed him into the mattress. He heard the chime of ten o'clock with his eyelids too heavy to raise. His breathing was rhythmic and deep, steady as the ticking on the mantel. He never heard eleven, or midnight.

It was the early 1850s, and times were good in Delaware. The work yards on the banks of the Brandywine River hummed day and night. The Du Pont

Company bought the Newcastle willow crop and burned it into charcoal, the least dangerous process in the company's treacherous manufacture of black powder and other explosives.

Free sometimes dreamed of being a powderman, but that work was for the Irish. Pap said farming willow to make the charcoal was as close as any black folk were likely to get to the excitement of making blasting powder. Farming and cutting willow in the warm May weather made Free itch with impatience, itchy to be full-grown and part of Pap's other work, treacherous as any powderman's.

When Free opened his eyes again, his father was humming below. Sunlight from the window and hatch played in the loft. The day would be bright. Free dressed and went down the ladder.

Nehemiah was at the fireplace. As full-grown as a man could be, he nearly filled the hearth as he pulled the iron skillet from the coals. His smile was kind, as if there had never been an argument, but Free went outside to the pump and privy without speaking.

"Eggs and hoecakes, son. Smell that?" Nehemiah said as Free returned. "There's just something about the smell of breakfast. Eat up. We got us a full day. I'll bring the wagon round soon as we've finished."

Free shrugged. "Pap, I can smell the dog chase. I know runaways came through last night."

"Can't smell a thing but peppered eggs, a seasoned breakfast. Take a seat. Day's a-wasting."

"How many came through last night?"

"Never mind. It's passed. Laws have changed since your mama died. Just the knowing of this work is a crime. The less you know in these matters—" Nehemiah sighed over the old argument. He filled their plates and sat down at the plank table that nearly filled the small room. "Son, you know ignorance'll keep you safe."

"I'm tired of being safe, and I hate being ignorant."

Nehemiah studied him long and hard this time, as if at any minute he might agree. Free stared back. Something was there in his father's brown eyes, in the set of his mouth. Watching Pap was like looking into dark water. Not the Brandywine, which tumbled this time of year and rushed its way along, but a still, shadowed pool, one that needed staring into to see what lay beneath the surface. Unconsciously Free took small breaths and waited, but Nehemiah just turned to the pitcher, poured them both some cider, and lowered his head for grace.

Twenty minutes later, Free was still at the table. "Son, it's time to think about something besides your stomach," Nehemiah called from outside on the buckboard wagon. "You'll make us late."

"Yes, sir," Free replied.

He flipped the last of his hoecake into his mouth and hitched up his overalls. Surely Pap knew he wasn't thinking about his stomach. He was still thinking about dog chase and hooting owls and moonless midnight trails that stretched from the Newcastle willow trees north, under the patch of stars that the runaways called the Drinking Gourd.

"Sorry," he mumbled as he scrambled up beside his father.

Pap didn't seem to hear. Behind them thickets and woodlots formed a border between their farm and the homestead of their Quaker neighbor Matthew Prescott. Ahead the trees and undergrowth bordered their own vegetable garden and the distant willow groves. Despite his impatience, Nehemiah kept the reins slack in his hands and stared out at the deep, green woods.

Free waited on the seat. "Pap?"

His father finally looked at him. "Sorry, son."

"What's out there?"

"Nothing but willow waiting to be cut."

If he squinted, he could just make out white patches through the trees, glimpses of the Prescotts' fresh laundry snapping in the breeze. He followed his father's glance. Pap's ears were sharper than a hound's nose. "You're looking for more than our willow. How many runaways have come through our farm?"

Nehemiah suddenly put his hand on his son's knee. "Many, Freedom, not enough."

There were no written records for this secret work, even though Nehemiah could read and write.

Matthew Prescott would know how many runaways Pap
had helped, but he agreed with Pap. "Nothing by the
pen," nothing that might get into the wrong hands.
Buckras were the white folk with power, and there
wasn't a thing they hated worse than abolitionists except freedmen who had once been slaves.

"Pap?"

Nehemiah seemed to shake off his reverie. "You're
the one's looking for more than he sees. Let's both of
us pay attention and get this load going. Why don't
you take the reins this morning?"

"You mean for me to drive Jack?!"

Nehemiah nodded. "This ole mule of ours knows
your ways, same as he knows mine. I'd say it's about
time you got the willow to the Hagley Yards on your
own. I'll come along this time, see how you do. Then
it's up to you."

"No fooling, Pap? I'll do just fine. You'll see!"

Nehemiah smiled. "There's no doubt."

They switched seats. Free took the reins, then
slapped them over the mule's rump. Jack began to
pull the loaded wagon forward.

"Good Jack." Free tugged the left rein, then steered
the mule carefully down their lane.

This wasn't the responsibility he'd been begging for,
but maybe getting willow to Hagley would help prove
to Pap that he could be trusted with the secret work.
Maybe Mr. du Pont would tell Pap what a fine job his

son was doing. If Pap heard it from somebody important...Free had to stop daydreaming as he steered Jack onto the Montchanin Road. After the sharp turn, he glanced over his shoulder. Not a twig had fallen from the wagon.

The wind shifted, and the air smelled of smoke from the stump-burning on Ellery McCall's empty lot. The Newcastles had started spring by helping to clear the property. It gave them cash money before the willows were ready.

"I'm wore out with cutting all this willow," Free said.

"Easier than hauling stumps. You be glad the powdermakers depend on the Newcastle crop. We'll be paid proper." Nehemiah turned on his seat and watched the back of the wagon for tumbling willow.

"I packed the wagon fine. We've hardly hit a bump."

"Didn't lose a branch. Doing just fine," Nehemiah said as he turned back around.

Free drove Jack in silence. When he couldn't stand it any longer, he looked sideways at his father. "What were you thinking back there, staring at the trees? Who's in our woods?"

"No one." Nehemiah had a way of closing down a topic with one sharp brown-eyed glance. He used it now, and Free stayed silent the rest of the way down the dusty pike, but his frustration burned as if he'd swallowed the skillet instead of the cornmeal patties.

At the approach to the Hagley Yards, Free steered Jack carefully off the main road and on to Wagoners Row, the lane just outside the gates. Here the spring air was full of the pungent aroma of axle grease, wood shavings, and varnish from the shops that lined this entrance to the powder mills.

As he sucked in a deep breath, alarm leaped in his chest. Ahead on the right, the Prescotts' plain, covered buggy pulled out from the cooper's shop. The harnessed mare turned and headed slowly over the ruts toward the Newcastles' mule. It was a sure sign of something.

Free glanced up at his father, who was suddenly all frown lines and squint.

As the buggy stopped, Nehemiah tipped his broad-beamed straw hat. "Well, good morning, Miss Liza."

Beneath the covered buggy and her wide plain bonnet, thirteen-year-old Liza Prescott's blue eyes were bright, but her expression was grave. "Good morning, Mr. Nehemiah. Hello, Free."

"Hey, Liza."

"My brother's family is down with measles, and Mother and Anne have gone to Talleyville to help. Father sent me for our kettle. The handle needed repair." She glanced left and right at the bustle of activity. "Father says to tell thee there's no shipment of wool, but we've new potatoes to spare. Thee can expect a bag or two in exchange for the repair of the harness."

"Potatoes. Mighty kind of you. You'll thank your folks?"

"Surely." Her blue eyes sparkled. She touched the rim of her bonnet, and Nehemiah tipped his hat.

Free scowled as Liza headed back down the lane. "Something's wrong. You never meet with the Prescotts 'cept at our place."

"Wasn't meeting now, son. Miss Liza just happened along."

"With tales to tell. She ain't but six months older than I am, Pap, and she knows more about what goes on right under my nose than I do," he whispered.

"Miss Liza Prescott's a white man's child, Freedom, and this wouldn't be the time or place to be forgetting the difference." Nehemiah slung his arm around him.

Free nudged his father's arm away. "Aw, Pap, your whole life's secret. Shipments of wool, new potatoes. All that hat-tipping when any Prescott comes by. If you can trust me with this old mule, you can trust me with other things."

"Son, those *other things* ain't a matter of trust."

To continue, Free would have had to raise his voice over the rap and clang from the blacksmith's forge, and he knew better. As they passed it, half a dozen men strained as they pushed a brand new Conestoga wagon from the shed into the daylight.

"There's a beauty," Nehemiah said. "She'll haul a lot of blasting powder."

When they were out of earshot, Free muttered, "Sure could haul a lot of other cargo. I could handle those reins. I could transport a whole shipment of wool every night, Delaware into Pennsylvania. I could take them right up to the Lion's Paw, if I had to."

"Child, that's what they call Canada, and it's a sight further than the state line we're living on. I should have named you Persistence instead of Freedom. Keep your mind on willow work."

"You got plans for our willow money tonight, Pap? Will we be storing those new potatoes overnight?"

Free didn't expect an answer and he didn't get one. He got *the look* again. They were too close to the bustle of the powder mills to continue. He'd pushed Pap as far as he'd dared.

Ahead, the willow yard was as busy as a marketplace. There were yapping dogs and yowling babies. Soot-faced charcoal-burners came up the hill from the river side mills. They collected the willow that women and children unloaded, stacked, even stripped and peeled if needed. It was the most white people Free ever saw in one place.

Nehemiah put his arm back around Free. "If it

cheers you any, think of your willow work as helping out. These are sorry times. We got a whole country out there opening up. New states and territories in need of roads, canals, rail beds, who can guess what else? We got the du Ponts wanting all the willow we can grow to make the blasting powder that's needed for that work."

"Our cash crop, Pap. You've always been proud."

"I take no pride in our cash crop helping settle territories that do nothing but spill blood over whether they're to become free or slave states. Seems fair that we use the money for better purposes. It makes our other work possible."

Nehemiah looked at his son. "Your sweat, your effort—You'll be driving this wagon from now on, right here to the mills."

"I guess that's better than nothing," Free replied. "It just don't feel like helping, is all."

Free managed to keep his mind on the willow for the rest of the day. May afternoons were long, and he worked alongside his father in their grove, which grew in the damp flood plain on the banks of the Brandy-wine. A tree could only be shorn of its branches every three or four years. Nehemiah had planted enough to rotate the harvest, guaranteeing spring income nearly every May and June.

By the time they began to lose the light, Free had sawed, collected, reached, bent, and lifted close to enough for another willow delivery. Every muscle in his body was complaining. He dragged the ladder across the open meadow to the tree that he meant to start on in the morning.

"Can't wait to jump in that old crick," he said as they quit for the day.

Nehemiah dusted off his hands. "You wash up at the pump tonight. Crick's running hard, and it's still cold, to boot."

"Just one dip, Pap!"

Nehemiah surveyed the meadow and the woods that separated their property from the Prescotts'. "I'll wait for you, then."

"Pap, I'm nearly growed."

"So's you keep telling me. All right then. One dip. Chores and supper need your attention." He picked up the tools and left to wash up and start their meal.

Free glanced into the woods as he skirted the edge and went to his usual spot at the riverbank. In spring shade, a beech tree hung over the water. Its roots clung precariously to the grassy slope, which was eroded by years of floods. Free watched the Brandywine rush over the rocks as he stripped off his homespun. He thought about driving the next shipment of willow by himself. He thought about Liza and "new potatoes."

Suddenly a small breeze played at the back of his neck. Gooseflesh rose on his scalp. He glanced quickly at the thickets again. Barely a leaf moved. He turned around and jumped for the creek before his imagination sent him scurrying. The water shocked him. He shrieked, but it felt good to be cooled off.

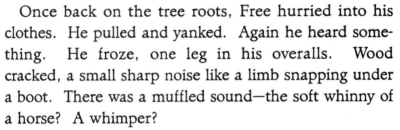

Once back on the tree roots, Free hurried into his clothes. He pulled and yanked. Again he heard something. He froze, one leg in his overalls. Wood cracked, a small sharp noise like a limb snapping under a boot. There was a muffled sound—the soft whinny of a horse? A whimper?

Free shivered and started for the cabin. Under his homespun shirt, his heart raced. He felt watched. He wished Pap hadn't taken the hatchet. He wished he were as tall as his shadow that the setting sun stretched across three rows of newly set potato plants. Once he reached the neat rows of greens, he forced himself to look back. Nothing had followed. From the closest tree, two squirrels chattered. Overhead a turkey buzzard drifted.

The Newcastles' two-acre vegetable plot lay between the willow grove and their few farm buildings. There were hardly more than sprouts in most of the rows. Free spotted Pap out back at the pump between the cabin and the barn, his back just visible as he washed up for supper. Still, Free's shoulders prickled.

He kept walking, but the gooseflesh rose all the way down his spine. He forced himself to laugh. Here he'd begged and nagged Pap all morning about helping out with runaways. Some stationmaster he'd be if he let his imagination play tricks on him with the sun still shining. He swallowed his fright and headed for the pump, determined to look as though there were nothing on his mind but his appetite.

"If I ain't about to starve," Free said with forced brightness as he reached his father.

"Bossie's waiting, son. You milk her; I'll make some biscuits to go with supper." He grinned. "Seems to me you're always on the edge of starvation."

Nehemiah brushed at the droplets of water still trickling over his arm. His bare back was a crisscross of angry scars, welts as familiar as the smile lines etched at the corners of his eyes, welts Free was never comfortable looking at.

The boy had dim memories of scars on his grandfather, too, but they had been tribal patterns on the old man's cheeks and forearms, awarded for honor and valor by the elders in his native village in Angola, before he'd been sold. Both were constant reminders that his family had had another life, one Pap now helped others escape.

Free left his father and went into the barn. Their cow was tethered in her stall. There weren't many who brought their animals indoors from spring through early fall. He suspected it was a signal, but Pap never would say.

The bucket filled with warm, frothy milk as Free pulled on Bossie's teats. It was boring work, and his mind wandered to his father. Pap had stared—hard—at their woods as they'd left for the willow yards that morning. Liza Prescott had said they could expect new potatoes. Couldn't mean anything but more run-aways. Maybe it had been a whine or whimper he'd heard by the creek. Runaways might be hunkered in their woods right this minute, waiting for nightfall. If he couldn't get answers, he'd just put the clues together himself and draw his own conclusions.

Straw drifted from the loft overhead onto Bossie's rump. At the moment Free looked up, a screech split the evening air. He jumped, knocking over the milking stool as a blur of orange fur landed at his feet. The barn cat shrieked again and tore off in pursuit.

"Dumb mousers," Free muttered, but his heart sank as he looked at the tipped pail. "Darn! I ain't got the brains God gave a turnip. The cats'll think it's Christmas dinner."

"Careless. Ain't like you, son," Nehemiah said as Free arrived at the hearth empty-handed.

"Stupid cat would've spooked you, too, Pap. Jumped right out of the loft, right to my feet."

Nehemiah patted him. "Chasing his own dinner, no doubt. Fill the pitcher at the pump. Water'll have to do."

When Free returned, his father had ladled out two bowls of stew and plates of greens, just picked and rinsed. They sat down, and Nehemiah bowed his head. "Lord, You gave me a heap of healthy willow this season. This bounty'll make many mighty happy."

Free stole a glance at his father. Who was going to be happy? The Hagley foreman, who'd get more willow to make more blasting powder? Their Quaker neighbor, who was probably fretting over the message Liza and Pap had shared? How about runaways out there somewhere? Were there more on their way? Was the Newcastle farm safe? Free watched a droplet of water slide down the spinach leaves.

"I expect you have something to add, son, while we have the Lord's attention."

The aroma of stew made his stomach growl like distant thunder. "I'm grateful for the wages the extra willow will bring. Lord, You show Pap who's to get helped by it." He glanced once at the ceiling. "And if You see fit, show me too, seeing as Pap won't never think I'm old enough. Amen."

His father coughed and gave him *the look.*

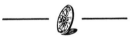

An hour later, Free had thrown kernels to the chickens and was in the enclosure slopping the hog. He looked from the yawning shadows in the barn back across the yard to the low light in the cabin windows. Night was settling in, and the anxious feeling pressed on him, tight as a rawhide lace.

At night his shins ached. Growing pains, Pap said, and sometimes rubbed them with herbal ointment. Free's denim overalls pulled shoulder to crotch when he worked, and they were new since Christmas. Boy-to-man kind of growing, Pap said. Free itched with it, as if his own skin were a size too small. Boy-to-man, and so far all he got was the responsibility of driving Jack to the willow yards. Free sighed. He guessed it was something. Better than nothing, but not by much.

He finished with the hog and had nearly finished with his mental complaining when he heard a soft whistle as he rinsed his hands at the pump. It came from behind the privy, at the edge of the woodlot. Free lowered the pump handle and listened to the rough tune, clear in the dusky light.

A runaway! Sure as he recognized the notes, somebody was signaling. His first impulse was to run and fetch Pap. No. He'd see to the fugitive himself, get his name and where he'd been last, evaluate his condition. He'd scurry the slave into the barn for safekeeping, then he'd go for Pap. Surely Pap would make him part of the night's adventure after that.

Free whistled back, primed the pump in his best nonchalant manner, then sauntered to the woodlot. Soon the sky would be no brighter than the woods. He had to clear his throat to keep his reply from spilling into a high-pitched tremble.

"Evening, Freedom."

His pulse jumped. Liza Prescott stepped from the path, no lighter than a shadow herself in her plain gray Quaker garb. Blonde as she was, barely a hair peeked from her black bonnet.

"So it's you," he said.

"Indeed. Who did you think I'd be? It's thee gave me a fright." She held out a basket. "I've brought thee some bread, fresh baked and more than we need."

Free cocked his head and whispered. "*Fresh baked and more than we need.*"

"Yes. With Mother and my sister away, Father and I thought..." She paused. "Freedom?"

"You bringing new potatoes, too, later tonight? You

can trust me with a message to Pap."

Liza laughed. "All I need trust thee with is the bread, silly. It's for thee and thy father. To eat, Freedom. It's not a coded message."

He frowned. "That's all? You talked about new potatoes this morning. I know that means runaways."

"I also talked about the kettle handle. It's repaired. That means we can simmer stew." Liza opened the napkin and handed him the loaves. "Sun's down and I'm without a lantern. Father will think it's I who've run away if I don't get home." She patted the bread in his hands. "Bread for thee and Nehemiah. Truly."

"You whistled."

She shrugged. "Thee knows our ways. Music is a prideful thing, though I do love it. I whistle when my parents can't hear me. It's thy father's tune."

"And a signal for sure," Free grumbled.

"This evening it was only to keep away the boredom. Thee looks so disappointed."

"Well, I still ain't sure this is all the truth."

"Lying breaks a commandment, Freedom."

"Then I'll just take your old bread and be going in myself." He grimaced at his rudeness and muttered, "Don't take offense. Didn't mean nothing by that."

Liza smiled. "No offense taken."

Free entered the cabin and put the bread in the small cupboard for morning. He explained about Liza but left the rest alone. His disappointment and irritation kept him prickly and introspective until he realized his father was rubbing his back as he came from his bedroom with the Bible.

"Pap, you hurt yourself?"

Nehemiah straightened up. "It's an old ache. Don't you fret."

"From the whippings?"

Nehemiah sat in the rocker they kept near the window. "I reckon."

Free took his usual spot on the floor, tonight away from the heat of the dying fireplace embers. "You never say how...or why."

"I came by those scars same way all slaves do: something done, something I left undone. Don't much matter."

"From the Hammonds?"

"Yes."

"I'm old enough to know."

"You know my own mama and pap were in Maryland, owned by the Hammonds. They were a hateful bunch who had a place along the Choptank. We was all called by the name of Hammond. The Hammonds'd hit you soon as look at you; worked my folks to death, if you want my opinion. Lucky for me, they fell on hard times, and I was put on the block."

"And bought by the Talbots."

"Yep, down in Odessa. They were educators who came to believe no man should hold another as property. When old Massah T died, he freed all his slaves. I came to them trained in smithing, like your grandpap. Mr. George Talbot was a professor. Book smart, but didn't know one end of a hammer from the other. I shared my skills, and he taught me the proper way with words, spoken and written."

He raised the wick on the oil lamp and smiled. "I can't say which of us had a harder time learning, but we both managed. I stayed until I met your mama and it was time to start my own family."

"And that's why we ain't named Hammond."

"I carry their mark on my back. Didn't take to carrying their name as well, not for me, not for your mama, rest her soul. Surely not for my son."

"But you didn't pick Talbot."

"No, son, I took the name of the place where I first lived as a free man. Christiana Hundred in New Castle County's where we be living free. Liked the sound of New Castle."

Without further explanation he opened the Bible and read from Nehemiah, the book for which he was named.

The story wound Free up worse than ever. Telling family tales was like being given pieces of another part of himself. "Mama'd be glad to know I help in your

work," he said as his father finished.   He paused.
"Why is Bossie out some nights and in, others?"

"Summer's coming.   Warm enough.   Reckon Bossie
can go out tonight." Nehemiah closed the Bible.

"Warm enough for runaways to hide out there, waiting for sundown.   Waiting for a cow in the pasture.
Liza came by with the bread whistling through the
path.   Was it a signal, Pap?   Did she think I'd be you,
out there waiting for something?"

"Did she say that?"

"Well, no, but—"

"We'll be up with first light.   I reckon you better be
on your way to the barn, if you mean to see to Bossie
and the others.   Take the lantern and watch the straw."

Darned if Pap couldn't shut down conversation
quicker than a Hagley powderman doused an ember.
Free got to his feet and swallowed the urge to nag and
argue for details he knew he wouldn't get.   Under the
flickering light from the oil lamp and the clear night
sky, he crossed the yard.   He threw dinner scraps to
the hog and stared—hard—at the dark boundaries of
their property.   Who would walk these woods tonight?
Who was crouched by the creek waiting for a signal?
What would be that signal?   Who would give it?

He entered the barn.   "Guess the cats did have
Christmas dinner," he muttered as he tugged Bossie
from her stall.   The floorboards where the milk had
spilled were nearly bare.

First light teased Free awake. He lay on his pallet and smelled breakfast. No dog chase. No turpentine or pepper, just sizzling fatback and strong coffee. Pap was whistling to himself, anxious to get on with the day.

"Back better?" Free asked as he came to the table.

"Good night's sleep made all the difference." He slid a wooden plate across the planks. "Miss Liza's bread with some fresh-churned butter. We'll be sure to thank the Prescotts next time we see them." Nehemiah grinned at Free's expression. "Don't go reading hidden meanings into everything I say."

Father and son went back to the willows. Hagley Yards needed their saplings. It made Free proud. Despite Liza's admonition that too much pride was a worrisome thing, he liked thinking it over. As they walked across the wagon ruts and headed toward the Brandywine, he pictured himself on the buckboard seat, Jack's reins in his hands, saplings piled behind him as they arrived at the yards.

Free swung the hatchet and tried out Liza's tune. Nehemiah answered as he walked to the farthest trees. The ladder sat propped and waiting. Cash money. Of course, they made a little cash money in other ways too: stump clearing at McCall's, their surplus garden crop to his feed store and market, Pap's smithing here and there. Nothing paid as well as willow, however. Hard work, but it was worth it.

As the sun rose, the pile of saplings grew at the base of the trees. Nehemiah was at the end of a row when the familiar lowing of Bossie made them both look up.

"Sakes alive if she hasn't broken out again. Look there! She's nearly in the spinach rows. It's that fence, rotted through on the north side of the barn." Nehemiah sighed and wiped the sweat from his forehead with his bandanna. "Son, I got no choice but to repair that section. She'll trample our entire crop or else take it into her head to stroll clear to Wilmington one of these days." He looked at the height of the sun. "Your stomach must be about to order you in for a meal, anyway."

"Guess it was growling," Free called from atop his ladder.

"All right then. You finish up that tree while I get the cow back where she belongs. I'll mend that fence after we both put something in our stomachs."

Free waved his father off. The late morning air was still and blanket-warm on his shoulders. He hoped a breeze would pick up before the heat of the day lay down for good. His thoughts jumped from weather to work to Liza Prescott's bread as he finished the chopping and climbed back down the ladder to bundle the saplings.

"You, boy." Something hard poked him between his shoulder blades.

Free spun on his bare foot to face the barrel of a rifle. No sound had warned him. No crack of a branch underfoot, no whinny of a horse. No matter. A fair-faced, unshaven man stood no further than the butt end of the weapon. Another sat on horseback at the edge of the meadow, holding a second mare by the reins. Despite the warmth of the day, Free went cold as he had the night before. No matter what their business, one glance at them told Free there would be nothing but trouble, no further than the butt end of the weapon.

"You got an old man on the place?"

Free straightened and looked toward the barnyard. "Yes, sir. He's mending fences."

The man stabbed his rifle in the direction of the out buildings and mounted his horse. "We aim to pay him a visit. You included."

Free stumbled, but caught himself and straightened up, praying that his thundering heart wouldn't burst right through his overalls. The horses were quiet. There was no sweat on them, no lather, their hides cool as though they'd yet to be run. Not so much as a trot or canter down the Montchanin Road, he thought. These men had emerged from the woods. Camped? Spying? Free shivered. These two might surely have been what he'd heard yesterday. They might have watched his dunk in the crick. They might have heard his talk with Liza.

As he reached the yard, Pap appeared in the cabin doorway. His face was that dark pool again, placid, but his eyes seemed a whole shade browner.

He gave Free one clean, studied look. "Seems we're having company, Freedom. Come in."

"Pap?"

"You takes a seat at the table. Stay put no matter what. Hear?"

The men dismounted. They were equal to his father in height and dressed in simple homespun. Both fair faces were sunburned above a week's growth of beard. Both left their hats on. Both held rifles.

"This here a cabin of Matthew Prescott's? You be the sharecropper, Jeremiah?"

"No, suh. I be the owner, Nehemiah. Nehemiah Newcastle," he replied in the slave dialect he reserved for speaking to buckras or telling folk tales.

Astonishment crossed their features. "You ain't Prescott's tenant?"

Nehemiah slumped his shoulders and lowered his gaze. "No, suh. This be my farm."

"You a free man, boy? You own this farm?"

"I be proud to say I do, yassuh."

Free glanced at the three of them. *No, suh, yassuh* kept coming in the slow, humble dialect. Humiliation burned Free's cheeks, and beneath the table he balled his fists.

"If that don't beat all. You own that livestock?"

"Yassuh, I be a lucky man."

One of the men pushed his hat back, and a tuft of matted, yellow hair stuck out. "Maybe that luck's run out. You wouldn't be likely to mess around with no white abolitionists, got it in their heads to hide runaway slaves, would you?"

Nehemiah kept his glance on the floor. "No, suh. Don't know 'bout no runaways. I don'ts have nothing to do with em."

"What about this here Quaker neighbor, Matthew Prescott?"

"God-fearin' man's all I knows."

The blond man pulled a piece of paper from his pocket and held it up to Nehemiah. "We got a notice of reward for a slave, a buck named Amos Bentley, up from Maryland." He nodded at his partner. "This here's Jed Carter, patroller to the Bentley plantation."

Free held his breath. Patroller. The dreaded "patteroller" of a hundred slave tales.

"He's got information this Amos is coming up from Federalsburg, through Wilmington, maybe in the company of one of your kind. Ever seen a squat-sized woman, dent in her head, given to spells?"

"No, suh."

"Goes by the name of Harriet Tubman. You know

of a Quaker no-account named Thomas Garrett in Wilmington?"

"No, suh."

"If those two send him along, that puts Amos right to these parts. Wouldn't you say?"

Nehemiah shook his head. "Cain't say."

"We mean to track him down. Abolitionists been plucking our slaves—our rightful, legal property—like feathers off a Christmas goose." The man rattled the flyer. "Course you can't read, so it won't do me no good to leave this here."

"Let him keep it, for the likeness. In case Amos comes a-callin'," Jed Carter said as he poked his index finger into Nehemiah's chest. "You get word, any word, Amos is coming through these parts, or you get word that your neighbor Matthew Prescott's of a mind to help these lowlifes in Wilmington, you best hightail it up the road. We're stayin' at the Crossroads Tavern. You ask for Caleb Madison here, or me. You best bring us word, boy."

"Yassuh. I don't means to make no trouble for myself nor nobody else. I minds my own business. I reckons I got enough right here, keep me busy."

"I reckon you do." The man stepped forward. "To make sure you got nothing to hide, I'll just have a look around."

Free's heart jumped. Jed Carter poked the rifle into his chest. He held his breath as the sharp metal barrel pressed against his ribs.

The patroller frowned. "Freedmen ain't known for truth-tellin'. Your old man hiding anything?"

Free looked at his father, whose dark steady gaze never left him. "No, sir."

Caleb Madison shoved Nehemiah aside and rattled the ladder. "What's up there?"

"Loft, suh. My boy sleeps up there."

Jed looked at Nehemiah, then turned back around and poked Free again. "You, boy. Your old man ever hide slaves up there?"

"No."

"No what? You got manners? Stand when you talk to white folks."

Free stood. "No, sir. We work for Mister du Pont. We don't hide no runaways."

"Mister du Pont, is it?" Jed shoved the brim of his hat back and hooted. "First your old man tells me he's free. Now I'm to believe he's a powderman?"

Free's heart pounded so hard he could hear his pulse in his ears. He glanced quickly at his father for another dose of his strong, steady gaze. "No, sir. It's the Irish who work in the mills. We grow their willow. That's what I was doing when you...arrived."

"Willow." Caleb squinted.

"For burning, sir. Burned to charcoal for making the black powder."

"They pay you wages?"

"Some, sir."

Jed narrowed his gaze. "If I find out you're lying, and spending your time hiding what belongs to somebody else, you'll answer to me. That old man of yours ever take the strap to you?"

It seemed as though they wanted to hear that he had, so Free replied, "Some."

Caleb shoved him back onto his stool. "You think long and hard on the bite of that strap before you get mixed up in something treacherous and illegal as hiding runaways. I've half a mind to put you in my saddle. A short ride with me'll bring out the truth quick enough."

"You's heard the truth, suh," Nehemiah replied evenly.

"Maybe. You boys know what the Fugitive Slave Law is? You know it's against the law to shelter runaways? Fines, maybe prison for those who do. You know what an abolitionist is?"

Caleb pressed both hands on the table until the pads of his fingers went chalk white. "White trash is what they is, like your neighbor Matthew Prescott. Uppity Yankees breaking the law, thinking they can fool with other men's legal, rightful property. You ever stole somebody's horse, boy?"

Free shook his head.

"Out West that's a hanging offense. Any thief ever come by Mr. du Pont's and steal away his workers so there can't be no explosives made?"

"No, sir."

"You think them du Ponts would abide pirates coming for their powdermen? Stealing 'em away in the dead of night so there's no hands to make the powder?" Caleb pounded the table. "Well?"

"No, sir." Free flinched as Jed grabbed his arm and hauled him forward.

"Abolitionists is pirates," Jed said. "Cotton is king, but who grows the crop that's gonna wind up made into your shirts, boy?"

Free's elbow burned. "The slaves, sir."

Jed shook him free. "You and your old man'd be buck naked except for them field hands. Can't grow cotton without the bodies to pick it. Can't harvest it can't get it to market—to your Yankee mills. No cotton, no work, even up North. No tobacco, no crops, no food on the table without them hands. Right?"

"Yes, sir."

Caleb turned. "Don't neither of you never get messed up with white trash abolitionists. High and mighty troublemakers, think they can destroy the United States Constitution." Caleb lowered his voice. "Amos Bentley's worth two thousand dollars. Y'all're smart enough to figure the loss to his owner. I find out you're lying and you know the least thing about his whereabouts, ain't nobody makes a strap sing the way I do."

Jed turned to his partner. "Let's move along. Have a word with Matthew Prescott."

Caleb looked at Nehemiah. "You got papers say you're free?"

"Been free twenty years. It's in the will, suh, Massah George Talbot. Down in Odessa."

"The law's on my side, boy. If I say you're a runaway, it's got to be proved otherwise. There's a heap of 'missing property' hiding right out in the open by pretending they're free. Some been hiding twenty years. If I say you ain't free, there's no trial, no jury. It'll take a U.S. Commissioner to decide otherwise." He looked at Free. "I'm likely to say anything, if I think I'm being lied to."

Jed took the remains of Liza's loaf of bread from the table and bit into it. "Cabins and barns been know to burn in this part of the country. Right down to ash, and the livestock along with 'em. Can't hide other men's property in the ashes."

"No, suh."

"We're watching," he added with his mouth full. Both men glanced once more around the cabin and disappeared into the yard.

Neither father nor son spoke until the sound of the departing horses had drifted into the morning heat. Nehemiah bowed his head. "Lord, deliver us from the likes of slave catchers."

"White trash, pond scum patrollers," Free added with a sharp blink and a brush of his fist to his nose. He sniffed as he fought tears. "What rights they got coming in here, scaring us so bad? I'd sooner crawl in a rat hutch then get on a horse with the likes of those buckras." He swiped at his face. "I hate it when you act like you're a slave yourself, Pap."

Nehemiah looked at Free. "I don't much care for it, myself. Being a free black man can be a worrisome thing when buckras think we make trouble for slaves, for their way of life. They're just waiting for a reason to give me misery." He shook his head. "Remember this, son: it takes a smart man to act like he ain't."

"Can't think of anybody smarter than you."

Nehemiah grinned. "I'm guessing those old slave catchers will pay a call on Friend Prescott, then sneak around long enough to see if we're still in the willow. Once they see we're at work, they'll be on their way."

Free's heart sank. "Everything's upside-down. Everything's a mess! Even if we work willow all day, those old patrollers'll be at the tavern all night. They could make something up about you...take you away..."

His father hugged him. "I've been doing this work since before you took your first step. We have a plan some nights; some nights it goes for nothing."

"Ain't no man should own another one like he was property, like was a dog or a mule!"

"Moses worked all his life to free his people from bondage, right out of Egypt to the Promised Land. After all this time, I can't think the Lord looks kindly on one man owning another."

"I know He doesn't mind our work."

"Can't say as I'll ever be comfortable with all the truth-stretching it makes me do. Otherwise, this work suits me fine."

"Me, too, Pap. They won't find Amos, will they?"

"Amos Bentley came through night before last."

"He was the one? The dog chase I smelled?"

"He was here long enough for a meal and a change of clothes. He's well up on the Pennsylvania road, maybe to the other side of Chester County by now."

"Still on foot, Pap?"

"He's got a piece of our stump money going toward a train ticket."

"Out of Philadelphia? Out of New York?"

"Don't be asking what I'm not about to answer."

"Thomas Garrett's sending others from Wilmington, isn't he? I just know it."

"Son—"

"Pap, I'm old enough to know."

"You let me think on it some."

"On how I can fit in? How I can be a conductor?"

"Freedom, give me time to work this through. Men the likes of those patrollers..."

"Pap, I'm old enough." Nevertheless, familiar goose-flesh made the coarse threads of his shirt prickle. Under the patch of sleeve where the patroller had grabbed him, his skin was bruised and hot.

Nehemiah rubbed his forehead and forced Free to sit back down for their noonday meal. "Keep up your strength and keep up your normal routine. Ain't no patrollers going to make a mess of either."

When they'd finished, Nehemiah gathered the hatchets. "I'll walk you to the willows, but I got to get back to that fence. Put the visit out of your mind.

You're needed clearheaded out there. I don't want you cutting off fingers or toes on account of not being able to concentrate."

"You think those buckras will be as ornery and no-account to Friend Prescott as they were to us?"

"Can't say."

They threaded their way through the cornfield, careful to avoid the new green shoots in their regimental rows. As they headed toward the marshy meadow lined with willow trees, Free glanced over their shoulders. "You knew they were in these parts yesterday when we took the wagon to Hagley, didn't you."

"Didn't know for sure."

"Liza was telling you, too. 'New potatoes to spare,' she said. Here I was thinking new potatoes meant runaways. I thought that's who was watching from the woods."

"Don't dwell on it, Freedom." Nehemiah scanned the open fields and the thick dark trees.

"*New potatoes to spare.* Now I see what the meaning was." He shuddered.

"You mustn't think on it too much. This work's full of ornery white men trying to scare us. It makes their job easier if they think we all got the terrors."

"Pond scum," Free muttered.

As they reached the edge of the cornfield, a flock of crows rose from the rutted rows. Free stopped in his tracks and swore. When they arrived at the willows, he looked at his father and ached to ask him to stay. It would be the end of any hope of Pap letting him in on more important work, though. He held his tongue. "Where'll you be?"

"I'm working the section by the barn." Nehemiah looked at his son. "When you start to lose the light, you take a dip in the crick if you've a mind. Keep things normal, but no playing, no carrying on. You come back for cleaning up. We'll take what's cut to the yards. Mr. du Pont's waiting, and it'll give us an honest reason to get off the farm for a spell."

Nehemiah knelt on the dirt in front of Free. "Son, I'll be no further than the barn. There's barely a breath of wind and I got ears can hear you clear to the powder yards."

"Yes, sir. Ki! Pap, I ain't letting ornery slave catchers make me afraid on my own place."

"Good boy. Strutting around, puffed up like roosters, scaring children is what they do best. It ain't no more than smoke and the devil's design. Just do your work."

"I will." He looked at the woods.

"Holler if you need me. I'll come running."

"Yes, sir." Free watched the sun bounce off his father's shoulders as the older man wiped his forehead and adjusted his hat. "You holler, too, Pap," he called.

Without turning around, Nehemiah raised his hand in agreement and started back across the field.

Free began to strip the stacked saplings of their bark. Doing the stripping hiked up the wages they got for the willow. It also kept down his fear. The feeling of being watched made his skin hot. In his mind, a hundred pairs of eyes were in the woods, a hundred overseers and bounty hunters waited and watched with a hundred dogs ready to tear out over the fields.

He leaned back against a trunk. The nearest pollarded willows, cut back at the top of the thick trunk from years of being harvested for the making of explosives, were stripped of their branches. The second row had two years' growth of spiky branches sticking out in all directions. Their odd shapes were so commonplace that they no longer looked unusual to him.

Free tried to concentrate for safety's sake, but his mind wandered. At church Pastor Dunsmore had explained that the new law said runaways had to be branded or cropped when they were found and returned to their owners. Their ears were cut off to make examples of them. Free shivered at the thought.

The patrollers were lying. Nobody was plucking slaves away from their masters. Slaves were running off on their own, running with faith that hideaways like his farm and the Prescotts', and stationmasters and conductors like Pap and Friend Matthew, would get them safely up to the Canadian border.

Free stacked the green twigs and branches at the base of two trunks, then bent to pick up an armful. His work was slowed by constant glances: to the woods, to the creek bank, to the buzzards overhead and the saplings under foot. Pap would give him a tongue-lashing for sure if he continued to suspect every little whisper. Nevertheless, when the undergrowth bristled, he stopped.

"Who's there?" he called.

Nothing.

"Who's there?" he said again.

With a snap, the long, thin branch of a redbud dipped, rustling the new leaves around it. Squirrels again. The whole place felt queer on account of the patrollers. "Slave-catching, no-account griddle-greasers," Free muttered.

He worked his way to the riverbank willows, where the rushing water drowned out the skittering of squirrels and any other woodland creatures. It was nearly five o'clock when Free declared that he'd chopped enough for another wagonload. Hagley Yards would stay open in weather this good. They took the saplings day and night. In fact tonight, under the moon, women and children, even the powdermen, would be out in the grassy courtyard stripping bark.

He thought of supper. The thought of hoecakes and molasses made his mouth water.

Free dropped his hatchet at his feet. Pap would say he'd done plenty, enough for the delivery. He pulled the rawhide lace at his shirt front and stripped, then whooped as he held his nose and jumped off the roots of his favorite tree into the Brandywine.

He obeyed Nehemiah and kept the plunge to a quick dunk. There was no running back to the cabin. He had the hatchets and knives to carry, and sprouting crops to watch out for beneath his feet. Nevertheless, his growling stomach made him hurry.

"Hoecakes dripping in molasses," he moaned as he passed the beet crop. For a boy with no mama, he ate well. Pap made the best hoecakes he knew.

"Pap," he called out as he neared the cabin, "I'm about starving to death." He glanced at the repaired section of fencing. Pap had finished, too. "Pap?"

There was no answer. Above him the familiar turkey

buzzards circled lazily in the evening sun. The barn-yard was eerily quiet. By the time he walked to the open door of the cabin, alarm had raised the hairs along his arm. "Pap?" The boy tightened his grip on the hatchet.

The cabin was empty. At the window, the thin cotton curtain fluttered. The door to Pap's bedroom was open, and the quilt lay undisturbed on the mattress.

"Pap!" Free spun on his heel and was about to head for the door when a piece of paper caught his eye. At the far end of the table, the handbill lay with his father's chipped mug on it.

Free picked up the notice Jed Carter had left with Pap. There was a likeness of the slave Amos, along with his description and reward information. Now, however, at the bottom of the sheet, scratched in charcoal, someone had scrawled *Nehemiah 2:15.*

"They been back," Free whispered out loud. "They took Pap." He ran his hand over the likeness of Amos Bentley. *Nehemiah 2:15.* Free glanced at the mantel clock. Pap had written the time they took him, just past two o'clock. Hours ago, and no telling where they'd taken him. Maybe to the Crossroads Tavern where they were staying, maybe to the Prescotts. Maybe to jail. *Maybe they had accused him of being a runaway himself just to get even.*

Fear clutched Free's throat and choked the breath out of him. He stared at the flyer and tried to think.

The sun was already sinking, sucking light from the room. Night, soon. Very soon.

They had been bold enough in the daylight. Free couldn't bear to guess what two white men might do to Pap in the safety of darkness if they had reason to believe he had lied to them.

Amos Bentley's come and gone, Free wanted to shout. They'll never find him. It's done. He didn't shout, however; he sank onto the stool. They'd use fire to make their point. They'd burn the barn or do worse things, things Pap never talked about.

If they thought Pap was lying, they might press charges and have him jailed. Then they could come back to wait for the runaway. Free shot a glance at the empty doorway. What if they set up a trap? What if they suspected the Prescotts, too? Free jammed his eyes shut and tried to think. Of course they suspect the Prescotts, same as they suspected Pap and me, he thought. Me. Scary as it was, something in his chest warmed at the thought that he was included.

Behind his eyelids, he saw the patrollers as they'd been that noon, in the doorway, at the table, on horseback. Would men like Jed Carter and Caleb Madison let a black man go if he gave them information? If he confessed? Could they make him talk? Pap was a conductor, maybe even a stationmaster. One way or another, they'd see to it that he never helped another slave. That much was certain.

He ached to find Pap. But how? He tried to clear his head of fear and confusion. Where to start? It shamed him that he couldn't think. He might as well have been back under the Brandywine. He forced himself to concentrate. Pap needed him clearheaded.

Fear got right under his ribs and squeezed until he was cold all over. Pap, he cried silently. What would you do? Give me a sign. Clear my head!

Driving another load of willow to Hagley Yards would give him the excuse he needed to be out with the wagon in the dark. Soon he had the beginning of a plan. And probably, he reminded himself, it ought to start with a prayer.

He stood at the hearth and tried to think what might be a good enough prayer that God might hear it. Something from Matthew about loving thy fellow man? Something about David and Goliath? Free didn't have so much as a slingshot, and no black man, let alone a boy, was allowed to own a rifle.

He figured the Twenty-third Psalm would hold him in good stead if he could remember the words. He looked again at the likeness of Amos Bentley and reached for the Bible still beside the chair.

Nehemiah 2:15. The Bible. He slapped his forehead. Maybe Pap hadn't meant the time at all. Maybe Pap had left a clue. *Nehemiah 2:15.* Chapter Two, Verse Fifteen? Suddenly Free understood. Maybe Liza had come back this afternoon to warn Pap of something. Maybe he'd escaped before the patrollers had come and was hidden away in one of the underground stations. That was it. He was safe.

It could be. Anything could be.

Free opened the Bible to Nehemiah. He found Chapter Two and ran his finger along the print until Verse Fifteen appeared: *Then went I up in the night by the brook, and viewed the wall, and turned back and entered by the gate of the valley, and so returned.*

"He's run off to stay clear of the patrollers. He's somewhere by a gate, but he means to come home," Free whispered.

Free glanced around at the empty cabin, dim now in the low light. There was more to consider, and pieces of it worked their way into Free's reasoning. The first was a flat piece of fact: Pap would never leave for his own safety, never run off from anything, not from his child and not from his work.

Wasn't the magistrate's office right by the brook in Wilmington? The Brandywine ran behind that block of the city. Pap could mean for him to figure out that the creek was what he was referring to. Free had seen it a hundred times on market days. The Brandywine ran clean into town and out to the Delaware River.

"Viewed the wall," he whispered. That could mean he was in the walled building because the patrollers had him arrested and were trying to say he was helping runaways. *Gate of the valley... and so returned...*

Maybe Pap knew that Friend Prescott would help. Free nodded to himself and whispered, "He'll see Pap gets out. He'll see to it that Pap comes right up that old Montchanin Road to the pike and home. Be home before those old Hagley rolling mills douse their lanterns at first light." It could be.

It could be, and maybe Bossie would start mooing in English, and the hog would whistle and tell him what the signals were all about. Free scoffed at himself. Pap was in trouble. They were being watched. There was no use in pretending otherwise. He looked at his hands. He didn't know much, but he did know that Friend Prescott and Liza were his nearest hope.

He shivered, but stood up and kicked back the stool. No sense in worrying over what couldn't be changed. Save that energy for figuring out what he could influence. Small as his plan was, it was something to focus on, a dot on a horizon to keep him from losing his way: visit Liza's family.

Loading the wagon would have to wait. He laced up his boots, grabbed flint and a lantern, and folded the notice into the Bible. The quickest way to the Prescotts' was through the woodlot and scrub.

He only got as far as the new fencing when he stopped dead in his tracks. Dust rose around his feet. Their buckboard wagon had been dragged from the barn and now sat at a sickening tilt. Both front wheels were shattered, split to the axles.

8

Free ignored the knot in his stomach and the sweat
on his palms. The only way he was going to figure out
what to do was one step at a time. Can't run before
you learn to crawl, Pap was always saying.

He stared at the wagon. Sure as the creek rose in
the spring, it was meant as a warning. However, it was
a warning he was going to have to ignore. Daylight
had settled into dusk. Free's optimism died. Did he
really think the patrollers were honorable men? Did
Pap have real rights, as if he were white? Pap's message might have nothing to do with the magistrate's office, Wilmington, or a long walk home.

Free might have read it all wrong. Maybe it didn't
even have to do with Pap. Maybe the Bible verse had to

do with runaways, another slave. Maybe it had to do with another *shipment of wool* that Pap had thought he could move along without his son's knowledge.

All those nights he'd begged Pap to be trusted. All those times he'd nagged for information. Now he'd get some! Pap had laid it out in one Bible verse he was expected to decipher.

For the first time since Free had burst into the cabin, he felt something besides fear. Anger, hot and quick, took over. If only Pap had trusted him before, he'd know what to do now.

Free muttered Pap's words. "Ignorance will keep you safe." Not now. Not tonight. Ignorance made Pap's situation more dangerous and his own work a ball of confusion.

Wherever Pap was, was worry enough. The Bible verse only added to it. Free forgot the pounding of his heart and the sweat on his hands. There wasn't time for fear or anger. There wasn't time for anything but clearheaded common sense.

Was a *shipment of wool* due tonight? Due any minute, for all he knew. Bossie was still in the barnyard with the sow. Did Pap mean for her to stay out tonight? Chickens squawked and scattered as Free stared one last time at the broken wagon and forced himself to go into the dim barn. He struck flint. The lantern wick flared. This was what Pap would do.

Free waited and continued to clear his head. He

looked at the corner where he'd knocked over his milk
bucket. He kicked the straw with his toe.   Bright
lantern light cascaded over his boot.   He looked
around for the cats Pap kept as mousers.   As he kicked,
his foot caught the raised edge of one floor plank. To
his amazement, it shifted.   He angled his toe and
raised the pine board a few inches, expecting to see the
dirt the barn floor was laid on.   Hesitantly, he pushed
his foot into the blackness.   Air, damp enough to cool
his bare ankle, met his foot.   There was no dirt; there
was a room!   Free's skin crawled as if snakes had wrig-
gled up his pant leg.   He yanked his foot back.

He swallowed and forced himself to kneel on the
floor.   He lowered the lantern into the abyss.   A room!
Not much bigger than a privy, but there it was.   Quick
as he could, he put the plank back and shuffled straw
back over it.   No telling who was watching, waiting for
him to give something away.   Anger again, poker hot,
flooded his chest.   If those old patrollers were watching, his ignorance would lead them right to what
they'd suspected.

Free lowered the wick, and the lantern went out.
The Prescotts could tell him, true or not, that Amos
Bentley wasn't the only runaway coming through this
time.   Free hoped they could tell him about Pap
as well.

The sun was down, but not yet sunk enough to
throw the sky to blackness.   No moon yet.   Free left

the lantern in the barn. He brought Bossie to her stall and started through the woodlot and scrub toward the Prescott farm.

"Lordy, the dark never bothered me till now," he whispered. Those no-account patrollers could be anywhere, waiting for him, too. "Scaring the sense out of folks is what those old patrollers do best," he reminded himself. Free looked at the black stretch of woods ahead and wished he felt as brave as he sounded.

On either side of him, underbrush undulated with shadows that reached for him from the dark. He dreaded the night ahead. He pushed aside a pine bough. How many times had Pap wanted to tell his friends, to brag about the runaways he'd helped? There'll be nothing by the pen in these matters, he always said, nothing that could get into the wrong hands and endanger lives. Nothing by mouth, either, Free added silently with a sigh.

An owl hooted as he reached the far edge of the woods. A signal? He stopped and squinted at the dark. Nothing seemed disturbed ahead of him as gray lawn opened, defined by the hulking shapes of the Prescott bank barn, springhouse, smokehouse, and carriage shed. All were dark. The two-story homestead of Liza and her family was a mass of shadows.

"There's not a soul about," Free whispered. His heart sank as he crossed the grass to the courtyard side of the house. A single candle shone in the kitchen ell.

Sure as the moon would rise, a single candle in a dark house meant something. Guilt washed over him. Maybe if he'd been more clearheaded, he could have thought of another way to get to Pap, a way that wouldn't jeopardize his neighbors.

The owl hooted again. Free listened. From the dark barn came the heavy clippity-clop of a horse's hooves. He squinted and tried to make out the shape of Ginger, the Prescotts' mare. She's pulling the wagon, not the carriage, Free thought as he caught the squeak and groan of wooden wheels. The sound echoed in the cavernous space, then halted. A figure climbed down, tethered the horse, hurried toward him, then froze.

Free swallowed and stepped forward. "Is that you, Friend Prescott?" he said to the figure dressed in a cap, loose shirt, and rough-cut trousers. He stepped closer. "It's me, sir. Freedom Newcastle. I got some troubles on account of—"

The figure put out an arm. "Lower thy voice, Freedom."

"Liza!"

She looked back at the barn, then started in the opposite direction. "Follow me."

"Pap's gone, Liza. They—"

"Hush, Free. I know thy troubles," she whispered. She put her fingers to her lips and motioned as she moved across the grass and down the slope to the springhouse. Hinges squeaked and a blast of cold air hit them as she opened the door to the black, window-less interior.

Tin milk cans, crockery, and wooden shelves seemed to sway as Liza struck flint and lighted a lantern. She took off her hat and pushed at her hair. "Patrollers from Maryland paid us a visit, then returned with Nehemiah. They were bragging about ruining thy father's wagon, Free."

"That's why I've come. I thought your father—"

"He's been taken with Nehemiah into Wilmington, to the magistrate's."

Free leaned forward. "You sure? Your sure Pap's there, too? They ain't...done worse things to him?"

She nodded. "Have you eaten?"

Free shook his head. "I'm like to starve."

Liza offered him apples, a slab of smoked ham, and a tin cup of cider from the crocks and containers lining the shelves. "It's the way of the slave owners. If they have suspicions, they press charges. Sometimes they make them up; sometimes they're true. If Father is accused of harboring fugitive slaves, likely Friend Garrett will post bail in the morning. It's well past sundown. Thy father and mine will most likely be in jail this night."

9

"Jail," Free repeated as he chewed. "They said they'd charge him with being a runaway. Said it was their word over his."

"Don't give it a thought. There's no proof that he's a stationmaster, so they charge him with being a fugitive slave. Father made it clear that in Delaware there's many willing to testify to thy father's freedom."

"White men?"

"Certainly. Friend Garrett will be told. He's known to post bail in situations like this. He'll see no harm comes to Nehemiah, or Father," she added softly. "Even the Friends will want thy father where he is, maybe longer than overnight. It's safer..."

"Than where those old patrollers might have taken

him," Free finished for her bitterly. "Pap left a message. Nehemiah 2:15. It's a Bible clue."

Liza stared at him, hard. "Does thee remember the passage?"

"'I went up in the night by the brook and viewed the wall, and turned back, and entered by the gate of the valley and so returned'," Free said, then grinned at her surprise. "Pap and I memorize lots of verses."

"Indeed."

His pulse flew. He sat stock-still and forced himself to wait. Liza was chewing softly on her bottom lip.

"Free, Mr. Madison and Mr. Carter think Father's responsible for helping a runaway named Amos Bentley."

"He came through our place. Long gone by now."

The Quaker girl nodded. "Then thee knows?"

"Yes."

"As Friends, it's no secret we're abolitionists, but Father told them the truth. Amos hasn't been here. They chose not to believe him."

Free managed to relax a little. Jail was frightening, but if the likes of Thomas Garrett, the great conductor of the Underground Railroad, had become involved, then Pap might be safe enough for the time being. Now was the time to concentrate on other things, like the Bible verse.

Free shivered in the cold. "Liza, why'd you bring me in here? Where're you going with Ginger—in trousers?"

"You needed supper." Liza opened the springhouse door and pointed to a well-lighted building just visible further along the road. "Once they've made their claim in Wilmington, the patrollers will be coming back this way. They're staying at the inn. I have things to attend to."

"You mean the Crossroads Tavern? Liza, it ain't but spitting distance from your front door!"

She closed the door behind them, and they started back across the lawn. "Thee is not to worry. Father told them his family was at his son's in Talleyville. Except for me, truth enough. The house is dark."

"Except for the candle. Why aren't you with your mother? Where were you going?"

"Freedom..."

"Liza, the secret days are done! Don't you think I can figure a candle to be a signal? Didn't I hear owl hoots just now?" He chewed the last bit of ham. "Pap's left me a message I can't barely make sense of. All I know for sure is it ain't about Amos, since he's come and gone. You're pulling the wagon, and there's me, right smack in the yard. My ignorance ain't going to keep me safe now, and it might just mess up a heap of things for you. Don't you see I need to be part of this?"

Liza was quiet, as if she might be absorbing his anger, considering his frustration. "I was moving the wagon into the woods, in case the patrollers came back to ruin it the way they did thy own, Free. It's a troublesome job in the dark. Skirts get in the way. My trousers were my brother Jeremy's."

"Moving the wagon into the woods, or moving cargo?"

"I mean to move the wagon for safekeeping."

Free sighed. Lying broke the Ten Commandments, and despite the need for deception, Quakers had a way of skirting lies as if they were ruts under their wagon wheels.

He finally said, "Those old patrollers might just stop by here on their way to the inn. Pap says those men are known to do a heap of damage just to make a point. You need proof, come take a look at our wagon."

The two of them were silent, as if each were thinking over a separate plan. The air smelled of cool grass. Peepers were sounding, and the stream that fed the springhouse gurgled. Dusk had settled into darkness. Above them, the moon was rising. It was nearly full. Stars twinkled. Free struggled to temper his imagination with common sense.

"No sense in standing here scaring ourselves to death," he said to Liza. "I've got to think on Pap's message. Figure out what he means for me to do."

They both turned back to the barn. "Recite it to me again," she said.

"'Then went I up in the night.'" The sound of distant horses' hooves reached them. "You hear that?"

Free kept walking, but the sound was unmistakable. "Somebody's on the pike at a gallop. It's two sets of hoofbeats."

"Does thee want to hide?"

"Sure do, but wouldn't those slave catchers love to find me shivering behind some tree. They'd never believe I ain't up to something. Then there's no telling what they'll do." He pounded his fist into his palm. "We need a plan, and I ain't got the time to think of one. All's I know is we're getting out of here, Miss Liza, and we're holding our heads up while we do it." He snapped his fingers. "I know! I got the perfect excuse: I come to borrow your wagon. You give me that lantern."

"I can't be found with thee. If asked, thee's found no one home." Liza pointed to the kitchen. "Look, the candle's burned out. Go about thy business." She grabbed Free's sleeve. "Safe journey. Go back to your own barn. You and I can ride to my brother's from there. Have faith."

"I can't leave you."

She shook her capped head. "Thee is not to worry."

Free nodded, but hesitated. Surely she had a hiding place—dozens, maybe. Or was she going through the woods, where it was safer?

"Truly, Freedom. Do what thee must."

Before he could call her back, Liza disappeared into the open barn. The horse whinnied softly as the rhythmic sound of galloping horses grew louder. Free's hand was trembling so hard that the lantern light flickered.

"Wish I had a hatchet," he whispered.

At the entrance from the road, the horses slowed to a walk and the mumbled sound of male voices carried over the rutted lane. "Ain't I right, Caleb, lantern light, plain as day. Up there, by the barn."

Free listened to the squeak of leather as one of them stood in his stirrups. "You said pressing charges would keep them abolitionists in town. Now you're seeing lanterns? Jed, you ain't been right about much since we got here. Dead-end trails and wild goose chases. I'm hungry, wore out as a mule at sundown, and now we got to follow this godforsaken trail to Philadelphia tomorrow."

"If there's more Quakers to home, they're up to no good." The voices lowered to a mumble and continued as the men stopped the horses and sat in their saddles.

Free didn't wait for more. He hurried into the barn. In a flash, he was up on the buckboard seat. It was then that the unmistakable odor of turpentine and red pepper made his nostrils flare. Alarm, then anger, surged through him.

He wiped his palms on his pant legs and settled the reins in his hands as he looked over his shoulder. Hay was scattered in the wagon; an empty burlap bag lay in the corner. Otherwise it was empty. However, the 'stink' was faint, but unmistakable. That's what Liza had been doing, and still she wouldn't tell!

Sure as that moon was up, she'd been dressed in boys' clothes to move slave cargo. No wonder she'd wanted him to take the wagon before the patrollers got to it.

Free bit his lip and concocted a tale in case they noticed. "Turpentine. Friend Prescott's farming trick," he would say. "Put turpentine in your wagons, keeps critters from stealing crops when it's loaded for market." His heart was in his throat. The two patrollers wouldn't buy that story for a minute. He snapped the reins over the rump of the horse and drove the wagon out to meet them.

Right under the wagon boards, Free thought. Runaways, and he'd brought himself smack dab in the midst of it! For a moment, there was nothing but the sound of Ginger's heavy gait over the barn floor, then the cobblestone ramp, the easy groan of the wooden wheels as they left the safety of the dark space.

"G'yap," Free said. From the gait of the horse, he guessed there were no more than one or two slaves hidden under what was obviously a false wagon bottom. One or two! It might as well be ten or fifty.

Remember, he told himself, smoke and the devil's design is what those slave catchers are best at.

"Who goes there?"

Free steered the wagon close to the hog pen. The

stink of pigs and slop was enough to wrinkle his nose. He prayed it was enough to keep the patrollers off the scent of dog chase.

"I said who's there?" Jed Carter walked his horse to one side of the wagon with Caleb Madison next to him. "Well, look who we got! Missing your papa, boy?"

Free balled his fists so tight that his fingernails pressed his palms. "Yes, sir, but I reckon he'll be home come morning."

"Why's that?"

"'Cause he's innocent. Sir."

"And where would you be going?"

"The Hagley Yards, sir. Willow was due tonight. No wagon, sir, so I borrowed Friend Prescott's."

"Borrowed? Looks like stealin' to me. Full moon, empty house. Not a light in a window."

"No, sir. I ain't stealing it."

"Sure looks that way to me. I know a no-account horse-thievin' kid when I see one."

Fear made Free's ears ring. He was cold all over, cold as he'd been in the springhouse. Scaring boys is what they do best, he told himself. He lifted the reins as he concentrated on Pap's words. "Mr. du Pont will be wondering what's keeping me, sir. It's late already, and he's expectin' my pap with the willow."

Caleb leaned forward in his saddle. "Guess there won't be no Nehemiah Newcastle at the reins tonight.

You tell Mr. du Pont why your old man's in jail. See what he says."

Jed shifted. "C'mon, Caleb. We got better things to do than jaw by a pigsty. The stink's about to knock me outta my saddle. Let's take that look around and then get us some supper. Git on home, boy. Git!"

As the patrollers reined their horses away from the pigs and moved toward the barn, Free slapped the mare's rump with the reins. He hated leaving Liza, but if the patrollers got it in their heads to follow and found her in the wagon, things would be worse for her, for all of them. They'd make up more charges about Pap. No, there was nothing to be done but stand by his promise. It's what she wanted, and she was safer hiding.

Free sat straight as the wagon rolled under the rising moon. The road was hard-packed and rutted, something he'd normally give no thought to. Now, under the false bottom of the wagon bed, he could feel his precious cargo jostle and sway. Or maybe he could only sense it. There were two, maybe three in the back, he felt sure. Men probably, or maybe women. Maybe one was a child, likely to cry.

Free jammed his eyes shut and prayed. His imagination matched his pulse in speed. He needed to concentrate. He needed to stay calm.

Better slap the reins and hightail it into Wilmington. There were freed men in town. Friend Garrett lived right on Shipley Street. Liza's mother or brother might be there. There'd be grown-ups, black and white, to tell him what to do.

He repeated Pap's Bible message. Nehemiah 2:15. He carried the cargo already. He was meant for other work this night. Have faith.

The road around from the Prescotts' to the Newcastles' was far longer than the shortcut through the woods. It ran past the Crossroads Tavern, then through hilly farmland, so that grassy banks rose on either side for most of the journey. Thickets blocked the view. It felt like riding through a tunnel. Free had to pass under regimental rows of overhanging trees where the moon cast black branch shadows over the gray trail. Did stationmasters ever get used to the dark? Did they ever stop imagining patrollers in every shadow?

All those nights angry in his loft bed, Free had never thought about being frightened, not like this. He imagined risk and adventure and bravery. It hurt to admit that now he ached for daylight, for his cornhusk bed. For Pap.

Ahead, barely discernible in the moonlight, animals appeared at the crest of the hill. *Horses. No riders. Bounty hunters. Patrollers.*

Free yanked the lantern up as he approached. The animals froze briefly, stared, then scattered. Deer. He laughed weakly and tugged Ginger's rein.

The road curved. Ahead a row of brick buildings snuggled up against the road. Shafts of light beamed in long rectangles from the first set of windows, which Free knew as a meeting hall. Its front doors were open. Half a dozen horses stood tethered out front. Next to it was McCall's Feed and Market, where he and Pap sold their excess produce and helped Ellery McCall.

Embers glowed now from the stump pile. Free was used to the smell of smoke and didn't expect the horse to shy, but Ginger balked. She whinnied and pranced.

"Easy," Free muttered. He gripped the reins.

Men's voices rose and fell at the fires. When the weather was this good, more than the powder mills worked all night. The men paused as his wagon approached and watched him work to control the horse.

"G'yap." Free hustled Ginger on, anxious to pass white folks—anyone—this night who might have reason to question him. They were so close that his eyes watered from the smoke. He could see the plaid of the first man's shirt.

One corner to turn and then he'd be back on his own lane. Dark and empty as the farmstead was, he couldn't think of any place he'd rather go. Free tugged the left rein. The horse whinnied in protest at going any closer to the flames and raised its chin. Free tugged again, and slapped the rump. "G'yap, Ginger."

With a lurch, the mare cut the corner, crossing clear into the left lane in front of the feed store. She rounded the bend at right angles to the wagon, within inches of the hitching posts. The wagon frame leaned, rose on two wheels, and settled back down, scraping the edge of a picket fence. Beneath the boards came the obvious sound of weight rolling, shifting, and hitting the side rails.

"Trouble?" someone called out from the dark.

"Hey there, boy, we'll give you a hand if something's broke."

Free's heart sank as Ellery McCall crossed in front of the fence. He handed Free the now-dark lantern that had fallen from the seat.

"You shook something loose, I heard it shift when you came round that bend. Wheel's broke?"

"No, sir."

The man stood back. "Ain't it late for you being on the road? Ain't you Nehemiah's boy, helped with this clearing last month?"

"Yes, sir. I'm nearly home. Wagon's fine."

"I'll take a look."

"No, sir, no need. I'm expected home."

"Suit yourself. Get on home, then."

"Yes, sir. Thank you, sir." No more questions, sir!

He was expected home. Ellery McCall didn't need

to know it was a Quaker's daughter doing the expecting. It hadn't been a lie. Truth-stretching might just come easily!

A few minutes later, he swung the wagon into a curve and onto the lane to the cabin. Didn't he have enough on his mind without rebellious horses and curious white folk, even if they meant to help.

He didn't stop until he'd pulled into the barn. All the while he scanned his property for signs of Liza. Lordy, what if the patrollers had come searching through the woods? He swiveled and glanced into the straw-filled wagon bed and tried to decide if it was safe enough to call out to the cargo. "Ain't nothing broke," he said out loud.

The straw shifted, and the wagon boards creaked and seemed to rise by themselves. He gasped. With a single cough, Liza Prescott sat up, still wearing her cap and trousers.

"How'd you get—"

"There's nothing broken in the wagon except possibly me." Liza grinned. "I thought it safer under the wagon boards than hiding in the barn from those patrollers. Freedom Newcastle, thee needs a lesson or two on driving this rig. Thee hit every bump and rut on the road. And what a pace! I thought it'd take thee till Sixth Day to get here."

"Having to get your horse past McCall's stump fires didn't help."

She rubbed her shoulder. "I'm sorry. Listen to me! As if thee had any knowledge of a strange horse and neighbor's wagon."

"As if I had any knowledge you'd come along for the ride!"

"Thee can stop staring. Let me out. It's a coffin in here. And this night's not over."

Free scurried into the back and lifted one board. "Liza, I liked to die for wanting to talk with you! The minute I smelled the turpentine, I thought I'd brought runaways, on account of Pap's Bible verse."

"Thee nearly did."

"Where?"

"Nehemiah and Father were expecting another group. That's why I'm not with Mother."

"Ain't it always the same, your knowing everything and me left in the dark! If Pap had just told me, I never would've interrupted you—"

"Freedom, it's ignorance that keeps thee safe. Even Father agrees."

"Too late for that, Liza."

"Remember that thee and I are governed by separate laws, Free. Patrollers, even some sheriffs, think they need no laws at all when they suspect a black man of just about anything, let alone harboring runaways."

"But Pap—"

"Free, we don't have the night to talk this out. There's a group waiting."

"A group!"

"A family of five, sold on the blocks in lower Maryland to pay off debts, due to be sent hither and yon on Sixth Day. Planters from down in Louisiana bought the father. The mother was bound for Virginia, and the children to be house servants somewhere else."

"This whole way home, I thought for sure this wagon was full of runaways. I smelled the dog chase."

"It was. I had them all loaded and ready to go. I was doing fine, but I had to send them off the minute I saw thy lantern coming through the woods. It was impossible to tell if thee were friend or foe. The 'shipment' left by foot while I got thee into the springhouse."

"Then we don't need to worry about them? They've gone to the next place?"

Liza shook her head. "Thee has much to learn tonight. Our 'shipment' is waiting for thee, Freedom. Father wasn't able to tell me anything before he left. I was only going to take them to our meeting house."

"Center Meeting is a station?"

"Yes, but whether it's secure tonight, I couldn't say. Only thee knows which station is next, which is safe."

"Me! Pap's kept me stupid so long, I don't know what he means for me to do tonight." Free groaned as he thought about the jumbled Bible passage. "If he'd only let me help sooner."

"There are many, even Friends among the Meetings who disagree with this work, Free. Thee can not forget that for a moment." Liza climbed out.

The night air was sharp, and the uncertainty of what lay ahead kept Free stiff-backed and edgy. A dozen times or more, he'd run the Bible verse through his head. More times than that, he had looked over his shoulder.

The two of them walked into the yard. The moon hung bright and low and heavy with nothing to dim its glow as Free pulled Liza into the deepest shadows he could find. Under the overhanging maples, he recited the full Bible passage.

"'...*went I up in the night by the brook,*'" Liza repeated. "At the state line, the Montchanin Road follows the Brandywine. Thee can be sure we're to follow the creek."

"How far? *'And viewed the wall'?* Cripes, Mr. du Pont puts the powdermen to building stone walls when the mills ain't running. There's more stones than split rails marking pastures in these parts. We'll never figure out which one Pap meant. Can't we keep the runaways where they are? Can't they stay till our paps are back home?"

"Thee can never count on tomorrow, Freedom."

"Where are they waiting?"

"In thy barn."

He spun around. "My barn! With the patrollers—"

"The patrollers are after Amos Bentley. We can both pray they're thinking of nothing but him and heading north on a goose chase."

"But they might be still searching! My barn!" He remembered. "Under Bossie's stall! I spilled a bucket of milk. It disappeared too fast for the cats, even. Right through the floorboards, 'cept there was no dirt underneath. There's a secret room."

"Thee found it," Liza replied.

"With no help from Pap."

"And no need to lie, if thee had been asked. Thy ignorance—"

"I know, I know. Keeps me safe. Well, not tonight. Ignorance has got us both in danger."

"Nehemiah's taught us many things. What we don't know we can't pass on to the wrong hands. At thy farm, thy cow is the signal. If she's out to pasture, thy barn is a safe haven. No cow in sight means to go on to the next station."

"So that's it. Then you can bet I'm glad she's in her stall."

She laughed. "Bossie's good for more than milk. We had better see to our responsibility. This family didn't slip away from their cabins on Seventh Night."

"Saturday."

"Yes. That's the normal time, since slaves have the Sabbath to rest. Many runaways aren't missed till the next morning comes around and they're gone from the fields. By then they've had a twenty-four-hour head start. But this family didn't slip away. They ran from the auction block, right under the nose of their new owners."

Free turned as if the owners were galloping after him. "We better get moving."

"Have faith in Nehemiah's message."

"How can you know our guessing is right?"

"The stations are known, Free. Thee's brought thy father's message: *'And turned back, and entered by the gates of the valley.'* Does thee know where the Brandywine doubles back just before Chadds Ford?"

"Big Bend."

"There's a ridge, and below, the road cuts right through at Hill Crest Farm. It's lined with stone walls. It's a known crossroads."

"I know Hill Crest. It's the dairy. Pap's done some smithing for them. Took me along." He sighed. "Took me along, but not by way of moonlight."

"From there we take our cargo to the first station over the state line on the road to Kennett Square. Friends Isaac and Dinah Mendenhall live there in a big white house. Runaways enter by stone gates."

Free's teeth began to chatter. *"'And so returned.'* I can't wait till we get to that verse."

Over the peepers and the soft whoosh of the breeze came the pounding in his chest. The full moon was above the trees now and gave everything a tinny brightness. It made the lantern unnecessary—for himself or for anyone watching for his return—and added to the danger.

"If those patrollers are watching out for me, I wish they'd just come right up and show their snarly selves instead of sneaking around making my skin crawl," he whispered to himself.

He and Liza went back into the barn. Although his voice shook, he sang a familiar Gospel tune as a signal that all was well. So far.

It was darker inside, and even the familiar took on eerie shapes. A lantern would have helped, but he didn't dare light it. Instead he made his way to Bossie's stall. He eased her aside and sang again as he lifted the floorboards. Amid traces of turpentine, hay, and sour milk, one by one the family climbed from the Newcastles' shelter.

"I be Seth," the father whispered. "This be Lily and Baby Daisy." He turned and lifted two youngsters out as he named them. "This here's Benjamin and Nehemiah, called Nee."

"That's my pap's name," Free said, as a boy not much younger than he swiped at his tear-stained face.

"Where is he? What's takin' him so long?"

Free knew even the words *jail* or *patroller* would frighten them further. "Won't be Pap tonight. I'm going see you along."

"Mercy, Seth, he's just a boy," Lily whispered to her husband. "Looka there. He's no bigger than Nee."

"I've helped Pap plenty. You're not to worry."

Seth took Free by the arm and walked with him to the farthest corner of the stall. "Son, I know there's been some unexpectedness tonight. We're some ways off our route. The Quaker man, Mister Garrett, thought it was safe. He sent a message for Nehemiah."

"That's my pap. You give me the message."

"You is to see us to the stone gates. We's expected."

Inside Free, under the fear that had kept him shivering, that ember began to glow again. Liza had been right. Confidence. He could find the stone gates on the Kennett Pike same as Pap. "I know the route."

"We's to be met. We's to look for our Moses, Miz Tubman. She gonna get us from there right to the Lion's Paw. We come up from Newmarket on her word. Our Moses says God tells her the way. Turned around as this night be, you be one of His messengers. You get us on that route this night."

Free had to bite his tongue as he followed Seth back to the others. God hadn't given this Moses the full message if she thought Canada was just a day's journey from Delaware. Or maybe it was that she didn't want to discourage them. Didn't they know they had weeks ahead of them of nights like this? But how could they? No slaves had maps. No slaves were allowed schooling or any such knowledge.

The baby began to cry. "Dear Lord," Lily said as she tried to soothe her.

Liza moved everyone under the nearest window, and Free watched in amazement as she opened the grain bin. In the dim light, she pushed her arm into the feed and shook off a glass bottle. She handed the stopper to Free. He recognized the sharp licorice smell. Bellyache medicine!

"Paregoric," she whispered as she ministered to the baby. "It'll make thy little one sleep." She turned to Seth.   "Does thee have shoes under the turpentine rags?"

"Yes, miss. Mr. Garrett saw to it."

She grinned at Free's astonishment.   "Thy father keeps boots in here when needed. Ours are kept in the springhouse. It makes for cold walking sometimes." She handed a feed bag to Lily. "Slip Daisy into this. Nee, Benjamin, it's time for thy next adventure. All of thee, into the wagon."

"Will they fit?"

"Surely."

When the boards were laid flat over the hidden cargo, Free turned to Liza, "There's plenty of willow saplings all cut and waiting. Before we start, I'm going to fill the back. It's a normal sight this time of year. It'll be another lie, but anyone out tonight can think I'm getting this crop back to Hagley with your wagon. I'm supposed to anyway."

"Thee needn't lie. Our wagon for thy work is fine."

Although he hadn't lost sight of the danger, the ember in Free's chest had warmed him through with confidence. He was proud of all that had taken place right in his own barn, prouder still of thinking up adding the willow load to further disguise the cargo.

Once again he slapped the reins over Ginger and headed the horse into the moonlight. They passed the vegetable garden and reached the willows at a walk. Under the wagon's false bed, no baby cried, no children whimpered. If all went well, they'd leave Hagley Yards to the south and head north up the road to the Hill Crest Farm. From there Ginger would follow the lane to the pike. They'd deliver the human cargo in less than an hour.

Free glanced at Liza, sitting on the seat beside him. "If you don't look like a willow worker in that cap and shirt."

"Pity I don't have the Irish brogue to sound like one."

As quickly as they could, they loaded the wagon, just high enough so that the saplings and branches were obvious. When they were back on the seat, Free smiled. "Truth be told, Liza, I'm glad you're with me."

He was about to continue when the whinny of a horse made him spin. There, in the moonlight, coming from the road onto his lane were two horses in a walk.

"Ki! Don't they got better things to do by now?" He sat rail-straight and prayed as hard as he ever had in his life. Liza started to jump from the seat.

"Don't run," he whispered. "Lie down. If they've been watching, they've seen you in this light. If not, they'll think Ginger's taking the wagon of her own accord. Get your horse to move along, deep as you can into the shadows, near the creek. I'll head the other direction."

"Right to the patrollers, Freedom!"

"Just go, Liza, so they don't get wind of the dog chase. Go!"

"Free, thee can't—"

"Keep your cap on, and keep Ginger at a walk. Get going." He jumped to the ground and watched the Prescott horse pull the wagon. Well behind him down the lane, the riders slowed. Maybe they hadn't spotted him yet. Or maybe they were sizing him up. He bent back to the willow and tried his best to look busy. He listened to their muffled voices as the wagon moved away. Praying was starting to come easily. He prayed for the baby to stay quiet. He prayed for Liza. He prayed the patrollers had satisfied their curiosity.

Though he hoped they wouldn't, the shadowed riders swung back under the moonlight and headed toward the willows. Free glanced once more at the Prescott wagon, now nearly at the creek, and stood his ground, exposed as the pollarded trees under the bright gray light. He thought of the deer he'd startled on his way here, frozen for a moment, ears raised. Did their hearts slam against their ribs? Did they go all over ice and tremble before they dashed for cover?

Jed Carter was the first to speak. "Ain't nine o'clock a little late for working, boy?"

Free raised an armful of saplings. "Yes, sir, but I told you, sir, that's why I borrowed the wagon. There's a job to finish. Mr. du Pont's waiting."

Caleb reined his horse. "Little strange, ain't it, hauling willow this late in a Quaker's wagon? No lantern? Ain't it past your bedtime, boy?"

"Yes, sir. Got a job to finish."

He craned his neck. "Got some help?"

"No, sir."

Caleb squinted at the willows, then swung his riding crop. It cracked once against Free's shoulder. "You telling me I'm seeing things?"

Free's knees buckled and his ears rang, but he stayed on his feet, clearheaded. "No, sir. Mr. du Pont has explosives to make. He—" *Think what to say! Make it believable!* "He sent a fellow out to supervise. He expects the shipment tonight. I'm working for him's what I meant, sir."

"Some powderman's brat's out there? Maybe we'll have us a conversation."

"No, sir!"

Caleb turned back around in his saddle, arm raised again.

"It's the foreman's son, Mr. Alexis du Pont, sir, come to see I do my job, on account of your taking Pap. When I didn't deliver the willow tonight, he came out to see why."

"Blamed it on me, did you?"

"He was looking for an answer, sir. Liked to have my hide for being late," Free began again.

Jed ignored him and tapped Caleb with his boot. "Look here, Madison, I don't aim to get mixed up in the wrath of a du Pont waiting for his willow. Kid or not, he could make trouble. His old man comes round demanding explanations from us, we'll lose a day's tracking. We already got our own boss to answer to. We got our own business giving us fits. No need to wrassle around with another." He pointed down at Free. "You and your Mr. du Pont out there stick to willow work. Nothin' else."

"Yes, sir. It's all I meant to do all along."

"You mean to move that wagon tonight?"

"The mills run all night when times are good, sir."

"If you get it into your head to put yourself off this property, it'd better be nowheres but to them powder yards. Due south."

"Yes, sir."

"Don't expect your papa tonight."

"No, sir."

"We'll have one more look at that cabin of yours," Jed said.

Caleb leaned over. "We'll be out tonight, goin' over these parts, till Amos is found. And he will be found." Without warning he leaned down and cracked his crop again across Free's shoulders. "Now git!"

Pain raced through Free as he stumbled, then sank

on his knees into the saplings. Tears stung his eyes. He picked up the twigs and forced himself to walk toward Liza. Even in the dark, the stares from the patrollers froze his blood.

Finally, he heard them rein their horses and start off toward his cabin. He heard loud raps on his cabin door. It didn't take imagination to know that the knock came from the butt end of a patroller's rifle.

Free forced himself to concentrate on what lay ahead, not what the patrollers might be doing inside his cabin. *Five runaways.* If two patrollers had been sent to track a single man, Free could only guess how many might be looking for a whole family, every one of them worth money. Before long he might have two sets of searchers with ears sharp as a rabbit's looking for just what he was driving: a loaded wagon.

"I thought my heart would break my ribs," Liza whispered as she and Free loaded the wagon. "It's pounding like a churn into butter."

"Ki, if I don't know the feeling!"

"Who did thee say I was?"

"Alexis du Pont, looking for his old man's willow. He's near your age."

"Freedom, such imagination!"

The minute the patrollers cantered out the lane and

into the night, Free tapped the wagon floor and whispered to the runaways that all was clear. He tugged Liza out of their hearing. "Those buckras could turn up anywhere tonight if they take it into their heads to follow us. We fooled 'em once, but it won't work again if they get a sniff of this wagon. Won't work if they even see the wagon north of this homestead. And what if another bunch comes looking for Seth?" He lowered his voice even further. "We got us five runaways, Liza. Can you guess how big the bounty on them is? Who knows how many are searching for them already? There's only one way to get this cargo to the next station. We got to walk 'em there."

"That's too dangerous. It would take hours! We can hide here, in thy barn. We've done it many times."

"Liza, Seth said there's a stationmaster waiting for them. Moses, they call her. We're to get them there by way of Pap's message. If she gets it into her head to come looking when they don't show up, she'll likely wind up caught herself. We're walking. They're counting on Pap. I mean to see his word is kept."

"With no cover, along the road—"

"We'll follow the crick. I know that old river. There's wide banks, and willow groves further along...Most places there's no road in sight. It's far enough away so if the baby cries or we need to rest, we won't be spotted or heard. Ain't you always telling me to have faith?"

"So I am, but Freedom—"

"Come on, then. Put your faith in me. Pap left clues in that Bible verse. This is what he meant for me to do. First thing let's get this wagon back in my barn, empty. If the patrollers come back later, it'll look like I made the delivery and returned. I'll tend to Ginger and the wagon. You get the runaways straight out to the pines. I'll get some warmer clothes and some charcoal for you."

"Charcoal?"

"To darken you up, Liza. In this light, you'll stand out like a Prescott signal lamp. I'll be right back. Git!" Free grinned and pointed through the trees. "There's a clear spot with a big old beech tree hanging over the crick. The roots are all bare. It's my swimming platform. I'll meet you there."

The night pressed on him as he and Liza helped the family. Under his ribs, the knot of fear began to loosen. He had a clear plan in his head and a route to follow. Maybe this was how it was for Pap. Maybe there wasn't time for being scared when so many were counting on you.

Lily was shivering, and the boys were frightened. "I'm too tired," one of them said.

"Hush now, got a long night ahead," their father whispered.

Liza led them off. Time felt suspended as Free drove the empty wagon to the barn. As fast as he could, he put Ginger out to pasture and hung the bridle and reins on a barn peg. Eerie rectangles of moonlight shot through the barn windows onto the floor at his feet. He looked back once at the hulking shape of the wagons and left for the cabin.

Ginger whinnied in the pasture. Even Jack, their mule, was agitated. Free looked at his cabin. Smoke still hung in the air, sharp, too close for McCall's Feed Store.

"Pond scum! Lowlife snakes!" He jumped the split-rail fence and ran across the barnyard. Nausea gripped him as a faint orange glow flickered through the single window on the east side of the cabin.

Free tried the door, jimmied shut by the patrollers. Pap's hand-wrought thumb latch was cool. No fire near the door yet. When it wouldn't budge under his hands, Free gritted his teeth. He ignored the pain in his shoulder and threw his weight against the planks. The hinges groaned as the wood split and he stumbled into the room.

A single trickle of flame streamed from the fireplace to the ladder propped against the stone hearth. Like a bright, evil vine, it had climbed one rail and half the rungs. Above him, in his own loft, Free could hear the fire crackle as it devoured his straw pallet bed.

His nostrils flared. He swore and threw his arm across his eyes against the smoke. The unmistakable stench of kerosene made him cough. He kicked aside

Pap's overturned lantern, which was propped to look as though it had fallen.

"Pond scum! Griddle-greasers!" With both hands, he grabbed the ladder by the unburned rail, knocked it first to the floor, then dragged it into the yard. His fear settled into something closer to caution. His ears felt huge as he listened for layers of sound: the dreaded hoofbeats over the crackling flames. His nose burned. His skin prickled. Under his shirt, his shoulder ached from the patroller's twice-swung crop and his own lunge against the door.

For the moment, the fire was contained in the loft. Not counting the baby, there were six able-bodied people as close as the creek who could help. Hope smothered the last of his fear. Together they could get this fire out. Together they could save his few precious family possessions. Under this roof was everything he and Pap owned, all trace of his family.

He and Liza and Seth and Lily and the boys...Surely before the flames ate into the floorboards and broke through onto the roof, they could smother it. Quilts and blankets, water from the pump...

It had only been seconds, but Free felt as though he'd stood there for hours. As quickly as the plan popped into his head, he forced it to ashes. Stationmasters didn't risk the lives of their cargo. The runaways' lives were already in jeopardy. Not even a burning cabin was reason enough to involve them in something that would bring them out in the open.

Tears, mostly from the smoke, ran down his cheeks. Wasn't there always some need lying deeper than what he saw on the surface? Pap was always telling him that, and now he could see it for himself. Before the flames drove him out, he made one rush into his father's room.

He fumbled in the dark, coughed, and threw open the chest at the foot of the bed. With one lunge, he filled his arms. He grabbed a smaller tin box from the bottom. Back out in the main room, he took the Bible. As he stooped, flaming straw felt from the loft. It drifted to ash on the hearth. Soon it would be the ceiling falling. Soon the whole loft would be engulfed.

Free's throat closed up. It was too hard. The lies, the crack of the riding crop, the fire. He was raw with tension and exhausted by decisions. Think! Choose! Lie! Hide! Since dusk his mind had raced, and there seemed no end in sight.

There was just enough room in his hand to grab a cold piece of wood ash to darken Liza's face, or the mantel clock. The ceiling joists were already groaning. Without a glance back, he took the ash, left, and ran across the dusty yard to the barn. There wasn't time to do more than empty his arms on the top of the grain bin. The family quilt, the Bible, the sweaters and shirt for the runaways, the tin box of his mother's, all tumbled in the moonlight.

He picked up Nehemiah's Sunday-go-to-meeting-jacket. Free rubbed his face into the sleeve. He drank in the familiar feel and smell of the worn fabric. He thought about Pap's Bible stories: Daniel in the lion's den, David standing up to Goliath. He wished Pap were there right now telling him one.

"I'm going," he whispered into the jacket. "Things have worked out different. We got sidetracked, Pap, but we're on our way." His throat was suddenly hot. Tears stung his eyes. "You'll be proud of me. Mamma would be, too. There's no cause to worry."

Free gathered what he needed and rushed into the night. He dodged the ruts and the open vegetable garden, his vision nearly obliterated by the dark and his tears. At the edge of the corn rows, he stumbled and blinked to clear his eyes. A steadying grip on his arm kept him from falling. He leaned into a solid wall of shoulders and chest.

"Pap?" His whisper broke.

"It's Seth, son. We smelled the smoke. Miss Liza figured it to be the work of them patrollers. No flames broke through yet. All of us working could beat it out."

Free swiped his eyes and looked up at the man, who was nearly as tall as his father. "We were meant for other work tonight. There's a long road and a stationmaster waiting. I mean to see that come morning you're well on your way to the Lion's Paw."

The group was huddled among the tree roots at the spot where he'd jumped. As Free handed out the sweaters and shirts, he acknowledged that the cabin was burning, but told all of them that his possessions were safe in the barn.

"Barely a breath of wind," he said to Liza. "It'll spook the livestock, but the flames won't jump that far. I figure the barn and the animals are safe."

"Freedom—"

"It's done, Liza." He handed her the wood ash. "Smear your face. Moonshine'll light you up like Mr. du Pont's rockets on Independence Day."

"Ain't that ole moon the brightest thing," Lily said as she put on the extra sweater and adjusted the sack with her baby in it. "No bigger than a coin, but lightin' our way. There's the North Star sittin' right over that ole design they calls The Drinking Gourd. Heaven's mapped our route."

Free leaned over to Nee and Benjamin. "From now on, it's back to being quiet. If you need to talk, you tug on my sleeve."

This is it, he told himself. The journey had begun. This was real—what Pap did, and the Prescotts, and the woman they called Moses. Dangerous as any powderman's task. Risk, adventure, bravery charged him with energy. There was just enough fear to keep him alert.

He grinned at Liza. Her face was now as dark and shadowed as the rest of theirs. In her brother's shirt and the rough-cut trousers, her blond hair tucked under the cap, even he wouldn't have recognized her. He tossed the cinder in the river. The usual spring gurgle and rumble of the swollen creek smothered the sound as their bodies broke branches and brushed through the undergrowth. The ground ran from damp to soggy as they tramped. He never turned back for a final look at the cabin.

For an hour, they snaked through the scrub. They tramped over skunk cabbage and spent narcissus. May mud caked their shoes and mixed with the dog chase. The river cut through hilly countryside that rose and fell in an exhausting pattern. Where the bank was wide and flat, they hurried along, but often the way was brambles and brush, rocks and ridges. Low spots were filled with pools.

The air had cooled, and Free's feet grew damp, then cold. To count his blessings, he thought of how this route would be in the dead of winter. It was the only blessing he could think of. The way seemed endless.

Occasional houses appeared. Sometimes there was a distant window light on a hillside. Springhouses sat near the meandering streams that flowed from the creek. The aroma of curing ham from a smokehouse made Free's stomach grumble.

Still they tramped. They helped each other over obstacles, offered a hand or an arm. Fear gave way to fatigue. Benjamin fell and began to cry, but Seth stood him up. "There now," he crooned.

Free hadn't rested since noon, hadn't for a minute expected to feel tired or hungry. The river way was far longer than he'd realized, far colder and darker. His arm hurt where the patroller had pinched it, and across his shoulders bruises had formed over bone-deep pain. Did Pap ever feel this way? Was it ever too much?

He thought of his straw and cornhusk bed gone to ashes. He tried to envision sizzling hoecakes instead of sizzling floorboards. Liza poked him, and he stopped as the strains of fiddle music drifted to them.

Free crouched lower but kept them all moving. Where the terrain evened out, a barn came into view glowing with lanterns. Over laughter and singing, a voice was calling out dance steps for a reel. Free kept the group hunkered down as they sneaked past, covered by the rhythmic clapping and the thumping of dancers' boots.

Nee began to whimper.

"Hush, chile," Seth said as he picked him up.

"Me, too," Benjamin whined as he lifted his arms and sat down.

Free's shins ached from ankles to knees. He rubbed one as he glanced at the yard. More than a dozen rigs, from surreys and buggies to wagons, were lined up side by side.

As the crow flew or the horse rode, he'd brought his cargo nearly to the state line. But nearly meant by way of the road and a fast carriage. By way of the circuitous Brandywine—and six pairs of swollen feet—they had hours ahead of them. He glanced quickly at Liza, then turned to size up the horses.

"What is thee thinking?"

Liza's sudden question, so close to his ear, made Free jump.

"The boys are already cranky. Soon they'll be crying for real. The baby won't sleep forever. My legs are about to crumble under me. I'm thinking there's a quicker way."

"Freedom!"

"I'm not stealing. I'll borrow one of those rigs; bring it right back tonight. Heck, they'll still be dancing."

"And what if they're not?"

"I'll keep riding and leave it close by where the owner can find it. They'll think the horse got loose, is all." It was impossible to see any expression in Liza's smudged, capped face. "It ain't like I'm breaking a commandment. Ain't it the Quakers who say this work is following God's law? I figure He'll understand what I'm doing."

"God understands that thee is helping slaves escape, but what if the horse owner understands, too? Or the sheriff? Free, if thee is caught, thy name would be linked to thy father's. He would be charged." She pulled him to his feet. "Friend Isaac is not so far away that we can't make it as we are, on foot." She leaned closer. "Thee is needed brave, not foolish."

Free took a deep breath, then another. This work was what he'd wanted, what he'd begged Pap for, what Pap had tried so hard to keep him from. He rubbed his sore shoulder. He thought of Pap's scars, and Grandpap's. He had his own marks now.

Guiding runaways didn't seem so exciting any more. "You're right. We can't risk anything more happening to Pap. We'd better carry the boys." As Seth put Nee into a piggyback, Free reached for Benjamin.

Lily handed the baby to him instead, and slung Benjamin up behind her. "I be a slave, chile, been slinging grain sacks and lumber heavier than this little one since I was his size. You just carry my Daisy and sees us to Moses."

"I mean to," he replied. Liza patted his arm.

They continued in silence through another acre of brambles. The hills grew steep, and the river widened. Boulders lined the river and formed a ledge, making it easy to stay in the shadows. They all lost track of the time until the riverbank widened again to meadow. Ahead, a road swept down the hill on their left and crossed in front of them under a covered bridge that spanned the water.

"The Big Bend!"

Sure enough, the Brandywine snaked into an S. There it was, on their right, as it had been all night, then doubling back on their left. "Pennsylvania. Hill Crest Farm ain't far, now. We followed the brook, like the Bible verse says. Now we'll find the walls."

"Lord be praised," Lily whispered.

It was too soon be praising the Lord, but Free managed to find a spurt of energy. He adjusted the baby so her strap wouldn't press on his shoulder welts and bruises, then tried to make out the steepness of the bank under the bridge.

As he squinted into the shadows, the sound of scrambling came from above him, inside the bridge. Free's heart stopped, then thundered. There was a howl. Footsteps shuffled. The sudden deep, fierce barking of two dogs sliced the night air.

Nee screamed. His cry rose over the barking and

the water. Free turned in horror. Liza froze next to him. Seth clapped his hand over his son's mouth and shoved Lily between the boulders. As the runaways scrambled for cover, Free hurried forward, well away from the rocks.

Two hounds raced from the covered bridge out into moonlight, scattering stones that rattled as they tumbled down the embankment. They yapped as they charged along the dirt to where Free stood.

"Prince! Duke!" A figure appeared from the depths of the bridge and followed the dogs. "Who's there?"

Every inch of Free's skin prickled with sweat as he looked down at the animals, inches from his ankles.

Free turned once, saw that Seth and Lily had vanished, and took Liza by the arm. "C'mon."

"Who's there?" boomed from the bridge. "Show yourself."

Free stopped at the last patch of bushes. "Stay here." Without a word, Liza took the baby off his shoulder and slung it over hers. "It's me, sir," he called.

The man reached his dogs and stood with one on either side of him.

"I mean to show myself," Free called as he inched forward. He cringed as the hounds snarled.

"Duke!" The dog sat.

Free took another step forward and looked up at the tallest white man he'd ever seen.

"Why, you're just a colored boy! Sakes alive, if'n your scream didn't scare the stuffing outta me and my dogs. What's got you spooked?"

"Didn't expect the dogs, sir."

The man knelt and slung an arm over each animal as he glanced in Liza's direction. "Who you got with you—over there by that bush?"

Free turned slowly, acting as slow and dumb as he could while he concocted another plan. "It's my brother, sir. He's scared of dogs."

"What's he carrying?"

Free turned back. "Carrying? His belongings."

"What're you boys doing out so late?"

"Late?"

"You gotta repeat everything I say, boy? Mighty late for a child to be hanging around the crick. Dangerous, too. You fall in that rushing water this time o' night, you ain't likely to be found till you're drowned and swept clear into town."

"Yes, sir." Free nodded.

"You been camping out? You smell of woodsmoke and mud and who knows what all. How long you been out? I'll go fetch your brother."

"No, sir!" Free stepped closer and forced himself to pat one of the dogs. "That is, it'll make things worse."

"Worse?"

Maybe it was fear, or relief, or exhaustion; something rushed up through Free's chest until he was close to bursting. He bit his lower lip and willed tears to rise in his eyes. They came easily, and he let them slide over his cheeks as he choked on sobs. "Yes, sir. I runned away. Forced my brother to come along."

The man laughed and leaned back on his heels. "So that's it. Your old man's too hard on you? Your mama don't understand you?"

Lordy, he was sinking into a black pit of lies. "Yes, sir. Too many chores."

"Who's your pa, boy?"

Free ignored the question. "But we're going back. We were on our way home."

"Where, son?"

Where! Free wiped his eyes and swept the air with his hand. "Over there a ways. Not far."

"The Brinton place? You boys the tenant farmer's sons?"

"Yes, sir." His lies were stacking up like logs on a woodpile.

The man stood back up. "So you two are part of Lucas Jackson's brood? He's done work for me on occasion. Don't you recognize me? I'm Ed Frentz. I live right over there, across the crick."

"Yes, sir, now I do. It was dark, and the dogs and all—"

"You get on home then. Take your brother. It's nearly midnight, but I'll wager you've been missed already. You tell 'em Frentz sent you back."

"Yes, sir."

The man stood up and called his dogs with a whistle. They trotted peacefully at his heels as he sauntered back up the lane to the covered bridge. Free stood and listened to the hollow boot steps on the boards above him, nearly drowned out by the pounding in his chest. He went back to Liza, scrubbing away his tears as he went.

"Freedom! I was never so scared."

"You! This better be God's work, all right. There's enough lies hanging on my back to sink me to the bottom of that crick."

As he explained what happened, he and Liza watched the figure reach his house. They stayed long enough to hear the final calling of the dogs and the firm slam of a door.

With the group once again in tow, Free trudged over the final grass, skunk cabbage, and deer hollows. Both boys were sound asleep, dead weight across their parents' backs, their heads bobbing. Daisy woke and fussed, but Liza shifted her to a comfortable position and rocked her as they made their way.

On their left, the Montchanin Road appeared, parallel to them, nearly on the riverbank. After hours in the dark, Free's ears were as sharp as his barn cats' listening for field mice. He had to keep himself from whooping for joy when the riverbank widened to meadow. They'd reached the merger. Across the road, directly in front of them, stone walls were framed by granite posts: the carriage entrance to Hill Crest Farm.

"Nearly there! Nearly there," he whispered.

"Thee is right," Liza replied. "This time we can chance the lane. Walk near the edge, it's no more than a cart path. There's little between here and the station but pastures."

They passed the entrance and followed the lane, the stone wall on their right. Up the hill they trudged, single file, dark figures rounded by piggybacked children. The road sliced through the hill, open on the left to acres of crops. On the right, it was bright enough to make out the shapes of the dairy herd scattered and motionless around a distant barn. Still they trudged.

The hulking shapes of solitary trees no longer seemed scary. Free spotted the frozen silhouettes of another group of deer. He smiled. It seemed days ago that anything that harmless had frightened him.

He looked up. Above the open fields the sky danced with stars, millions, he supposed. They twinkled like June fireflies. Right this minute, those same stars shone over Seth and Lily's empty slave cabin; on the auction block in Newmarket; on plantation houses; on Irish powdermen's tenements and freedmen's barns. They twinkled over the willow yards at Hagley, the

Wilmington jail, and his burning cabin. Farther away than Seth and Lily knew, they were shining down on the Canadian border.

The little group had been in the free state of Pennsylvania since Big Bend. Did Seth and Lily know that not long ago this would have been far enough? Did they know that once they could have settled here and been safe? Did they know about the new law that said those that had done so could now be sent back into slavery?

Free found the North Star. He was no bigger than a speck of starlight. It was long past his bedtime. His shirt smelled of smoke, his overalls and boots of the mud; his legs ached. His stomach was hollow. What did it matter, one slave family on its way, when there were thousands left? What did he matter? He looked back at all of them.

Liza called it Inner Light, knowing a right thing, even when it was against the law. A single person could show the way; others would follow. Pap called it conscience. Except for the lies he'd concocted, Free felt just fine about his.

The lane rose, fell, and rose again. There was another springhouse, and the black shapes of tilled and, planted fields. Liza pointed to the dark mass of houses ahead of them. "The Kennett Pike is just out there. We'll go through the woods and come around to Friend Isaac's stone gates from the back."

"Can I believe my ears?" Seth said.

Liza smiled. "Indeed. This journey has but ten more minutes."

Free offered once more to carry one of the boys, but both parents declined. As he turned back to the lane, Lily groaned and pointed, "Have mercy."

A figure stood ten feet from all of them. Without shelter this time, the group stood still, exposed as deer in the empty field.

Although he would have felt a whole lot safer stepping into Seth's shadow, Free put his arm out to keep the others back. "Sir?"

The figure carried a walking stick and approached slowly. His rough-cut clothes were dark and plain, and his hat was down over his eyes. He was shorter than the man on the bridge by nearly a foot, but that did nothing to quell Free's fear.

So close. They were within shouting distance of the Mendenhall homestead. The figure pointed the stick at them. Then, in a woman's voice, the figure began to sing a soft, familiar gospel hymn. After a verse, she asked, "I expects you're Seth and Lily?"

"Moses!"

She wrapped an arm around Free, another around Liza. The hug was bone-crushing. "Praise the Lord. I found you. Friend Isaac and Dinah've been fretting all night. You're fiercely delayed. Word came about your fathers, and the Mendenhalls held out little hope for any of you this night." She dropped her arms and put a fist to her heart. "But gracious, didn't I know the Lord wouldn't let his sheep stray. He just sent them a different shepherd, is all. I told Friend Isaac and Dinah."

"Told them?"

The short black woman took off her hat and touched Free's cheek. "What that ole prophet Isaiah says: *'And a little child shall lead them.'*"

Lily pointed to the Mendenhalls' stone gate posts, sentinels at the homestead's carriage entrance on the Kennett Pike. As the group crossed the lawn, the back door opened. A couple stood in silhouette on the threshold.

The aroma of baking bread wafted into the spring air. Free ached to enter, to eat and sleep. He imagined a kitchen like Liza's: stew simmering; a washtub, maybe a change of clothes. A night's sleep on crisp linens, a real featherbed. A bed he might never want to get out of, a house he might never want to leave.

Instead he filled his head with thoughts of Bossie and Jack, the willow waiting in the Prescott wagon. There were places and things that needed him more than he needed this. And what if Pap did come home deep in the night and found him gone? No, he had to get on home. Soon.

As the group traipsed through the door, Free held back and stepped into the shadows. "Seth?"

The older man turned on the stoop. "Freedom, I owes you plenty for this night, for what you done for my family."

Free hoped he sounded like Nehemiah. "We help all we can. You just keep moving along. Your Moses'll know what's safe. I'll be leaving you now, things to tend to at home." He lowered his voice further. "Don't be mentioning my going to Miss Liza unless she sees I'm missing."

"Back to your cabin, Freedom? You stay in that barn. You been hero enough tonight. Don't you be fooling with that fire."

"Don't mean to." Before he changed his mind, Free disappeared into the dark. "Pap," he whispered twice as he left by way of the gates.

He hurried south on the Kennett Pike, along the shoulder, and watched his shadow under the sharp gray moonlight. It was a long walk home, but direct, nothing like the circuitous route he'd devised along the Brandywine. Nevertheless, by the time he cut east off the pike toward Montchanin, his legs felt like lead.

The Prescotts' Quaker meeting house marked the halfway point, a place to sleep—or hide—if need be. "Don't need it," he muttered as he limped closer. Free didn't intend to stop.

"'*And so returned,*' Pap. You got to, too," he whispered as he reached the fieldstone meeting house. The building was somber, its windows dark, the long, three-sided carriage shed deserted. Or so it looked. Free stumbled closer. His shins ached. Blisters burned on his heels. He sat heavily on the porch and hugged a column supporting the roof.

Another time, another night, he might lead a shipment of wool right along Center Meeting Road, right to this station. Closer, so much closer to home. He tried to keep his eyes open, but his head lolled and hit the post. He forced himself to stand.

In another ten minutes, smoke was in the air. He squinted into the dark for signs of flames. He'd lost all track of the hour, but figured it was after midnight but well before dawn. The cool air revived him, made his heart race as he pressed himself toward home.

He reached the lane and looked first out into the dark stand of willows. In his mind, he could hear the rhythmic thud of Pap's hatchet and his whistled tune as the branches tumbled. Free stood still and ignored his aching legs. When his throat burned and tears stung, he blamed it on the smoke and wiped his eyes on his sleeve. There were no flames. No crackling heat. The square, black shadow that had been his cabin was smoldering. He forced himself closer.

Free opened his eyes. Gray light was pulling shadows from the stall. He was in the corner, on a bed he'd made from the loft hay and Pap's quilt. He sat up as every muscle in his body complained. He was stiff all over. The light was gray. It was either dawn or dusk. He could have slept through a whole day, even two, if not for the chores.

For four days, he'd taken his meals at the Prescotts' because they insisted, but he slept in the barn to be ready. Pap would be home any time, he was sure of it. Friend Prescott had explained about magistrates and commissioners. He said that when the patrollers couldn't prove that Nehemiah had helped Amos, they'd charged him with being a runaway himself. They took him downstate to Odessa, where he'd been sold to the Talbots as a young man. Now it had to do with probate, wills, and looking into the estate of George Talbot to see about Nehemiah's being a free man.

"Pap's been free since before I was born."

"Have patience, Freedom. Thee has honest men on thy side," Matthew Prescott said.

Ellery McCall came by at a gallop the first day and

explained that he and his brother had tried to fight the fire but thought that both father and son had perished in it. The Prescotts had told him otherwise. Free didn't give him any more explanation, but accepted the offer of scrap lumber when the McCalls began their addition and the Newcastles were ready to rebuild the cabin.

Time crawled. Free delivered the willow to Hagley, returned Ginger and the wagon to Liza and cared for his livestock. On his second day back, he'd fashioned the stall into living quarters.

It rained. The charred remains of the cabin no longer smoked, but the whole homestead stunk of wet ashes and cinders. Free got so he could look at it without having to press his fist to his stomach.

"Soon as Pap gets back," Free took to repeating. A new cabin roof and a new set of clothes. Soon, soon, soon. Waiting and worry ate at him, and each plea from Liza to stay with her family made his temper flare like flint struck to light the lamp.

Now, four days into waiting, he stretched his sore shoulder and got up from the straw. It was dusk. He'd slept away the afternoon. The rain had settled into a mist that lay on Bossie's hide in minuscule droplets. She smelled of the damp as he brought her into the barn for milking.

When he'd tended the animals, Free left the barnyard for the vegetable patch. Looking at the weeds spouting between the crops washed guilt clear through him. He'd choose willow work and milking, even tending the hog, before weeding. Without Pap's pestering, he'd let it go, and it showed.

He slung the wooden hoe into the damp dirt. It stuck. He needed a proper supper first. Mud caked his boots. Maybe when he got back from Prescotts'. Maybe first thing in the morning.

He was about to sling the hoe a second time when movement at the lane caught his eye. A simple buggy stopped out on the road. A bent figure emerged. His right ear was bandaged and he took a cane as he tipped his hat. Free squinted. His heart jumped.

"Pap!"

As the buggy circled and headed back, Nehemiah raised the cane in greeting. He limped and Free charged, racing the length of their property. "Pap!"

Neither stopped until they were boot to boot. "What'd they do? What's that bandage? Why are you limping? Oh, Pap!"

Nehemiah smiled. Next to the wound, his face was swollen, but unscarred. "It's what they do, son."

"Not the magistrate."

"Patrollers. They got to figure a way to make their point." He opened his arms, and despite the pain in Free's shoulder, his father's grip was warm and ·omforting.

Free nuzzled his face against his father's shirt.

"They made their point here, too."

"The Friends told me. It could have been you in that fire."

A sob broke from Free's throat. "I had to let it burn. I had to choose, Pap. The others would have helped, but I couldn't have them out in the open."

"Hush, son. I know. Bravest thing I ever heard."

"And you?"

"I'm back. This ain't nothing won't heal just fine. There were charges brought, but none could stick. It's the patrollers' way—legal—to keep abolitionists from moving the slaves."

Free cleared his throat. "Well we moved 'em, all right. I figured out your note. We read the clues. Liza helped. She dressed up like a boy, and I made her put charcoal on her face so she wouldn't show so much. It took us so long. We were gonna come by wagon but those old patrollers—"

"Freedom, I heard all about it. 'Bout the most courageous thing two young'uns could do."

Free swiped his eyes. "Didn't I tell you? Didn't I say I could help?"

"More than once."

"We saw to the whole family, Seth and Lily. Three children too, Pap."

"You did a brave thing, and thanks to you the family's gone again, this time by carriage to Philadelphia and on up to the Lion's Paw."

"And the Moses woman?"

"Gone, too. No one asks where, and that's as it should be."

"Ignorance keeps us safe."

"Keeps her safe, too." They began to walk.

"I made us a place in the barn. Come see what I saved from the fire. Mr. McCall says there's lumber we can have, for rebuilding and all. The barn's just fine, Pap. Still just fine for runaways. For next time."

Nehemiah put his arm on Free's shoulder. "Son, I can't say there'll be a next time."

"But, Pap, I just got started!" Free turned and looked up at his father.

"We're being watched now. Suspected."

"They hit me, too, but I didn't stop. We had them fooled. In the dark they thought Liza—"

"Freedom, we've been beaten. We've been burned out. Sometimes a thing's done out of spite. You young'uns did fine. I did fine with the magistrate. But not finding proof, not catching us at what they suspected just stuck in the craw of those patrollers. When they suspect something and it can't be proved, buckras like them need a way to leave their mark."

Nehemiah ran his hand over Free's head, then pulled him close. "The barn..." His voice broke. "If you hadn't figured out my message...Lord, Freedom, it's the only place Miss Liza knew to go with the 'cargo'. Turns me inside out just to think how close you came to being caught in it."

Free felt woozy, but they kept walking. "But I did figure out the message, and we kept the cargo safe."

"That you did."

"Most everything's gone. Things are a mess, but we still got our cash crop."

Nehemiah sighed. "This morning I felt low as the ashes. The Quaker man who saw me home said we must remain optimists." He smiled again. "I reckon you're one."

"If it means I ain't quitting, then I am, clean through. Smoke and the devil's design, that's all—remember, Pap? We can't let two old buckras scare us away from what we were meant to do."

"Even with a cabin gone to cinders, and a night longer than most days, you want to keep at it?"

"We got willow. It'll get us cash. We'll build another cabin, maybe one with better hiding places."

"How'd I raise such a stubborn child?"

"Liza says we learn from example."

Nehemiah laughed. "So we do. This is my work."

Free straightened his shoulders until he was as tall as he could make himself. He slung his arm around his father and urged him toward the quarters he'd fashioned in the barn. "Well, there it is, then. I mean to help. Then when I'm growed, it'll be my work, too."

"Freedom, when you're growed, I pray there'll be no need."